The Strakhov plague!

Mack Bolan caught a glimpse of a white face in the crowd, the face of a middle-aged, balding man, swimming above the sea of Chinese heads. A terrible hatred snaked its way across Bolan's face—a hatred for his own fallibility and for the man who lived because of it.

The Executioner forced his body to move faster as he worked his way toward the target. Blood pounded as each step brought him closer to the man who had robbed him of so much. The crowd became mere background, his pursuit so consuming that he was impervious to the lives around him.

Bolan drew his big gun and took aim. With ice in his heart the Executioner knew that he would never be at peace until he had brought down Strakhov.

MACK BOLAN

The Executioner

DON PENDLETON's EXECUTIONER
MACK BOLAN
Fastburn

A GOLD EAGLE BOOK FROM
W RLDWIDE

TORONTO • NEW YORK • LONDON • PARIS
AMSTERDAM • STOCKHOLM • HAMBURG
ATHENS • MILAN • TOKYO • SYDNEY

First edition December 1985

ISBN 0-373-61084-X

Special thanks and acknowledgment to
James Lord for his contributions to this work.

Printed in Canada

To be on the wire is life.
The rest is waiting.

—Kurt Wallenda, after his
first time back on the
tightrope following his
family's fatal accident
in Detroit.

Dedicated to the memories of Charles Hegna and William Stanford, U.S. Agency for International Development officials murdered by hijackers at Teheran's Mehrabad airport.

"We shall know their murderers with the long memories of those who believe in patient but certain justice. Wanton murder of the innocent is terrorism that no amount of incantation can disguise."

— Vice President George Bush

1

"Forget the damn jogger," Colonel Molinz shouted across the room. "The man we want will be dressed informally to visit a relative."

Sergei Strassko did not take his eye from the telescope. "The girl could have alerted him," he said in a flat voice. "Our presence here could have attracted attention There are any number of possibilities."

"I say he is a jogger," Molinz announced imperiously. "Watch the road."

Strassko made a show of turning the telescope up the Chemin de la Côte-des-Neiges. Rush-hour traffic had just started in the fashionable Montreal neighborhood. The Russian senior agent knew there was nothing to be gained by watching the cars, but he pretended to do so until Colonel Molinz's attention lapsed.

Then Strassko once again directed the telescope toward the jogger. Strange, he thought, that the man should choose such a time of day to run. And in such weather. There was no precipitation, but the Christmas season had left the Montreal streets gray and wet with slush. The jogger's lower body would be soaked, and he'd be carrying five kilos of water in his shoes and pants.

Why does this man run outside and not on a track? Strassko did not ask the question out loud. He knew that Colonel Molinz would only answer by making the question the reason. "He runs outside because he doesn't run inside." The colonel would try to humiliate him with this very Russian answer, but Strassko was not so easily humiliated. Molinz was a dull man, quick to anger and eager to show his superiority to all those around him.

Too eager, Strassko thought.

Right now Colonel Molinz was showing the strain of remaining indoors on an observation job for the past three days. Molinz had been out of the field too long, Strassko decided.

He wondered why Strakhov had picked Molinz to replace the dead man, Vichinsky. He thought he knew.

Vichinsky had been ambitious. Too ambitious. Strakhov did not enjoy watching his junior officers for signs of treachery. Molinz was the perfect solution.

The colonel was competent in a crude, unimaginative way. And, Strassko knew, despite the fact that he was a bully and a bragging fool, Molinz was loyal to a fault.

It was not a fault Strassko shared.

The senior agent had long since decided that he was better suited for Molinz's job than Molinz was himself.

My chance will come, Strassko reminded himself. His eye followed the tracksuited figure through the puddles on the opposite side of the street. His right hand on the telescope's smooth white surface guided the gradual arc.

Strassko was impressed by the ease with which the running man picked his way over the slippery surface of the street. But the nagging doubt came back to him.

Why does he run outside? What is it about this man that makes me suspicious?

The runner's hooded sweat top could conceal a gun. Strassko only had to think this thought to imagine the outline of a big handgun—a Magnum maybe—that caused the fabric of the sweat top to fold as it did.

He had not run on the first day, Strassko noted. It was only yesterday and today that the jogger ran up the mountain and down again.

"Demeter, he's watching that damn jogger again," Molinz sneered behind him. "Take over at the glass."

Strassko remembered that one of the things most disliked about Molinz was that the dull-witted man used the word *glass* when he meant telescope. He offered the eyepiece to the giant who stepped up behind him, then took up a position at the headset.

"Anything?" he called through to the radioman in the girl's apartment.

"Nothing, yet."

"The girl?"

"She cooperates, but she knows her uncle is in danger."

"Can she hear me?"

"No."

"Use her to answer the intercom. Don't kill her unless she gets in the way. We can use her to persuade the uncle."

"Do you think he'll come today?"

Who knows? Strassko thought. The mail check on the niece's apartment had taken a whole year before it produced results. Even so, when the target finally contacted the girl, his note had only said, "I may come Christmas week."

"Today or tomorrow," Strassko said. He made it sound convincing.

Strassko could see nothing in front of him as he replaced the headset. The enormous brown-suited back of Demeter, the KGB enforcer, hunched over the little telescope and completely obscured the window.

Demeter was a freak, a huge Mongol easily six feet eight inches tall. The giant lifted his head from the eyepiece toward the photograph taped to the wall beside the window.

The photograph was an old one. It showed an Oriental man's face. The man's profession was easy to guess; he was wearing a stethoscope around his neck.

"He's here," the monster said without emotion.

"Who's here?" Molinz snapped. The colonel was smoking indulgently, seated on the only bed in the room.

"The target. The Japanese," Demeter said. "He just got out of a cab."

Strassko slapped a hand onto the enforcer's shoulder and pushed him away. At first he had trouble focusing, but it was the target for sure; he could feel it. Strassko had the headset in his left hand now. He was talking to the watchers. "A positive. A positive. The gray overcoat. No hat. He just left a cab. Take him slowly."

Strassko returned to the window and picked out two of the watchers leaving their places beside the niece's residence. It was going well.

Nice. Very nice. Do it softly, he said to himself as if the watchers, too, could hear his thoughts. Good, he thought as he saw them pause and wait until the old man had entered the apartment building. Very good.

A movement on the street diverted his attention briefly. He turned back toward the watchers before the significance of the diversion fully registered.

The jogger had returned. He was headed in the direction directly opposite the snatch. He was headed away from the Japanese toward this very hotel.

He was carrying a handgun.

It was some kind of Magnum.

Someone on the headset was chattering a request for instructions, but Strassko heard nothing. His mind was whirling at an impossible rate. No one else had spotted the jogger returning.

There was something very familiar about the track-suited figure that was now running flat out toward the outside staircase of the hotel housing the Soviets.

Strassko got an eyeful of the man's face before he disappeared beneath them.

He knew exactly who that man was.

The chatter in the headset continued, and Strassko now decided to respond to it. A small smirk showed on his reflection in the window, but it was invisible to the other men in the room.

"Yes. Yes," he said into the headset. "Continue as planned. I'm coming over." Without a word he replaced the mike on the table and left the room.

It's possible, he thought, as he raced down the corridor away from the direction the jogger would have to take. It's just possible that Demeter would be able to kill the approaching cyclone. Strassko had nothing against Demeter. In fact he wished the KGB enforcer the best of luck.

If he lives, Strassko decided, I'll promote him. Yes, he decided, taking the stairs to the street level three at a time, Demeter's chances were certainly much better than those of Colonel Molinz.

All Strassko had to do was complete the kidnapping successfully and wait for Mack Bolan to kill his superior.

Senior Agent Sergei Strassko was certain of his promotion. He ran lightly across Côte-des-Neiges imitating Bolan's own movements as he highstepped through the series of slush ponds.

Inside the apartment both Japanese, uncle and niece, were trussed up like Christmas turkeys by the time he arrived. *"Dobro,"* he congratulated his men. "Very good. Take them to New York."

"Sergei?" It was Janos's voice behind him. The radio-man seemed troubled.

"I can't get a response from Molinz or Demeter," he said plaintively.

"They'll come later," Strassko reassured him. "Let's get our fishes to the *master* chef, eh?"

Janos heard the accent on *master* and grinned. Between Colonel Molinz and General Strakhov there was a world of difference, Janos knew.

Demeter was hunched over the telescope again when the door burst open behind him. His head snapped up quickly, and he caught the reflection of the intruder in the window as he spun around to face the man.

Despite all the stories of big, slow men, Demeter was fast. His speed turned him in a fraction of the time it would have taken someone like Molinz.

Demeter was fast enough to identify the intruder from his reflection as he turned. It was the jogger. Strassko had been right, after all!

Molinz had been wrong. Now he suffered for it.

The dark-haired, tracksuited man fired into the Russian colonel's face. Twice.

Molinz collapsed backward on the bed as though his torso were the folding part of a tailgate that would never close again.

The intruder whirled toward Demeter. He, too, was fast. At least as fast as I am, the Mongol reflected. He shot Molinz first because my back was turned.

A mistake!

Demeter dived sideways into the arc of the turning man's gun, knowing the intruder's momentum would carry him too far.

As he dodged, Demeter hefted the white tube of the telescope in his left hand and scoped it toward the jogger. He heard the man's gun explode and felt the flesh of his left arm bunch and tear raggedly at the bullet's impact.

The telescope found its mark. The lens shattered against the butt of the big gun. The jogger's hand went bloody from the last two fingers as the weapon sailed away from him.

Demeter, too, was unarmed.

It is okay now, he thought, facing the intruder. Demeter had never met anyone who could stand against him in a fair fight. He allowed himself to relax a little. He flexed the muscles in his wounded arm and found they functioned well.

The intruder had settled into a battle crouch. He was favoring his gun hand. He saw the slight movement in the Mongol's arms as the giant relaxed. The man's arms lowered a fraction of an inch, and his elbows drew together a hairsbreadth.

He attacked.

His strong fingers made a deadly V. Demeter had no time to avoid the blow, but he did not lose his eyes. The fingers glanced off the smooth stone of the Mongol's cheek and came away bloody. He could feel the wetness wash down his face and trickle to the corner of his mouth.

Demeter continued in the spin that the blow had caused him to begin. His right leg snapped in a roundhouse kick that connected solidly and sent his opponent crashing through what remained of the hotel-room door.

Demeter saw the man's head connect with the door frame. He was not finished completely, but he was stunned and on one knee as the Mongol entered the hallway to deliver the coup de grace. The crouching man did not look up at his approaching assailant.

He has lost, Demeter decided. I will be quick.

He did not get the chance. .

Crouched on the green broadloom of the hall, Mack Bolan had spread his hands beside him.

From Demeter's angle, the other man's exaggerated need to steady himself was an admission of defeat.

He approached the Executioner quickly. Bolan studied the carpet in front of him until the booted feet of the giant came into range.

Mack Bolan pivoted, kicking upward and out into the giant's solar plexus. He felt the satisfying crunch of the connection and knew the Mongol had lost even as he came out of the upward kick and tumbled free.

The blow from the door frame had really cost him. His head spun as he came to his hands and knees and turned himself to face the fallen KGB man's body.

He watched the man's diaphragm, hoping he had not used too much force. Bolan needed him alive just a bit longer.

"Your spine is broken," he told the dying man in good Russian. "You feel nothing, but I can change that."

"Torture is so messy," the man wheezed. Bolan was startled by this unexpected attempt at humor. He examined the man more closely. A shudder passed through his enemy's body. The hands at the Mongol's side fluttered for a moment. He was sweating feverishly and his eyes strained to see Bolan's face, but he could not move his neck and the Executioner was outside his field of vision.

"What do you want?" he rasped.

"Greb Strakhov."

"Executioner!"

"Uh-huh."

"Show me your face, Executioner." Bolan moved closer. His head was already clearing but he was still on all fours. His face was very close to that of the Mongol's. He noticed the man's neck had disappeared. He had seen that before. Fluid from the spine flooded the flesh of the neck

and made it swell. A man with a broken spine looked like
a freak born without a neck.

"You are a pig, Executioner," the man said.

Bolan's face went hard. His eyes glinted with the black
light of death. Then he grinned.

"You understand?" the man asked.

"You have no fear." The Executioner nodded.

"No fear. No. You can't torture me."

Bolan nodded. His head was completely clear now and
he was on full alert. It was critical that he understand the
Mongol completely in order for him to get what he wanted.
The man was talking to him out of a need. Not a need to
protect himself but something else. *What did he want?*
Bolan wondered. What would I want if this was me?

The Executioner looked at the Soviet agent's broken
body and understood.

He wants to die, Bolan thought.

"Give me Strakhov and I'll kill you," he said.

"Get your gun," said the man called Demeter.

It was that easy.

2

Out the starboard porthole, the black towers of Manhattan scratched the northeast corner of the horizon as the freighter *Tito I* edged down the New Jersey industrial channel.

Vesh Slovincik heard a noise behind him and whirled toward the corridor. His shirttail was pulled up above the flab of his belly, exposing a money belt, which he was still strapping on.

"What?" he demanded angrily. The figure at the door was in shadow and Vesh's anxiety was plain.

"It's me," said the voice.

Vesh relaxed visibly. It was the wimp, Manfeld. No one ever worried about Manfeld. "What?" Vesh said again.

"Look," the tired little man said, casting his eyes anywhere but toward Vesh. "I've been thinking about your offer. I can use the money. What I mean is...it's still okay, isn't it?"

Vesh scowled at him. Nothing Manfeld ever said made sense. He never completed his thoughts. Sentences became paragraphs and paragraphs became whole books. But they were nonsense. A salad of incomplete thoughts. It was sad to think about.

Vesh had known that the man would be unable to resist his offer. At first Manfeld had declined to smuggle the jewels because he was scared. Vesh had anticipated that, too.

Now that he had changed his mind, Vesh would put the screws to him.

"I can't pay you as much as I promised," he said, tucking in his shirt.

"You said $4,500. You promised," Manfeld whined.

"I overestimated," Vesh told him. "All I can afford is $1,500."

"You'll make $100,000 from those diamonds."

"That's only the gross," Vesh said with a smirk. "Besides, it's not my money. I'm just the—" he searched for the English word "—I'm just the *director*. I get a percentage."

"It's *my* risk," Manfeld protested.

"Take it or leave it," Vesh told him. "Don't waste my time."

Manfeld's face turned away but Vesh Slovincik detected the curt nod that told him he had won. He opened a drawer on the radio table and withdrew a money belt like his own. One that obviously contained fewer diamonds.

"You knew I would agree?" Manfeld asked in amazement.

"No," Vesh lied. "I just wanted to be ready in case you did."

Manfeld nodded again. It was clear that he wanted to believe the smuggler. "What do I do?" he asked.

Vesh groaned inwardly. He had already explained the plan twice. "Get off before I do. Clear customs and wait at the rendezvous. If you're stopped, say nothing. I'll get you a lawyer."

Manfeld stood in the shadow beside the door and fumbled with the money belt. Vesh looked away. It will be better for Manfeld in jail, the smuggler thought savagely.

At least there he won't have to feed himself. Someone will do it for him.

Later Vesh stood on deck watching the line of seamen file into the customs shed as they disembarked.

Manfeld was among the first off the ship. Through the window of the shed Vesh watched the nervous little man stumble over his answers. Vesh could not see the INS officer's face, but he could hear the American voice demand that Manfeld submit to a strip search in another shed.

Vesh watched as Manfeld was led away. There were tears in the small man's eyes.

Good, Vesh Slovincik thought as he checked the fit of his money belt. Now it is safe for me.

He had known all along that the little man would not be able to carry off the smuggling job. At first Vesh had even considered notifying customs that someone was smuggling. But he had decided it was unnecessary. Manfeld had given himself away.

Now the customs officials would search the other personnel less thoroughly. Vesh hefted his rucksack and his pea jacket and stepped confidently onto the gangplank.

Next stop New York, he thought.

JAMES LOVELL WAS LATE.

Vesh waited in the rented car across from the New Yorker's brownstone for hours, wondering where his contact had gone. It was not like Lovell to miss an appointment. The businessman was untrustworthy and weak—Vesh knew that. But he also knew that in the past Lovell had always behaved like a professional.

He'll screw anybody for a dollar, Vesh thought as he stared at the entrance to Lovell's brownstone. That much was understood. But Lovell wasn't the kind of person to make you wait *before* he took advantage of you.

There's got to be a reason for this delay, Vesh told himself.

Finally a cab pulled up to the door of Lovell's home, and the businessman emerged. He was carrying an attaché case and a club bag. Vesh honked at him while Lovell fumbled with his house keys. The thin, blond man seemed a little drunk. He stared hard into Vesh's windshield before recognizing the sailor with a nod and a wave.

"It's dark," he told Vesh as he got in the front seat. "I thought you were a mugger."

"You should carry one of these," Vesh told him. He produced a palm-sized gun from the pocket of his pea jacket. Lovell blanched.

"No need for it," Lovell told the seaman. "The kind of people I do business with have slicker ways of taking your money."

Vesh nodded. From the little he knew about Lovell, he knew that much was true.

Lovell ran a finance company in one of the immigrant neighborhoods near the Red Hook. It was little more than a legit loan-sharking outfit that lent money to bad-risk clients, then bled them while the interest compounded on the original capital.

It was a sweet deal, Vesh thought. At one time he had envied Lovell.

Lately, however, Vesh knew that things had been bad for the New Yorker. A drug dependancy had eaten away most of the man's cash reserves. It had also done more than that. The cocaine that Lovell liked so much had weakened his judgment. He made one bad deal after another until his finance company was kept alive by Lovell's overpaid bookkeeper. A real artist.

Now, in desperation, Lovell was financing Vesh's diamond operation. The sailor had been pulling this smuggling scam for years but with Lovell's money he could increase volume one thousand percent.

"I'm going to drive down Seventh," he told the New Yorker as he started the car. "The diamonds are in a money belt under your seat. This time the shipment is light." Vesh turned sideways to catch Lovell's reaction.

"Light?" the man asked.

"Incidental expenses." Vesh smiled, thinking of Manfeld.

Lovell nodded, thinking that Vesh had bribed an INS officer.

"Did you bring the money?" Vesh asked him. The sailor was turning right out of the mid-Seventies onto Central Park West. As his eyes turned toward Lovell, he noticed a look of concern pass over the American's face.

"Y-yes. Right here," Lovell said, patting the club bag.

An alarm sounded at the base of Vesh Slovincik's spine but his face remained impassive. When Lovell produced a penlight and jeweler's lens to examine the stones, Vesh took a cigarette from his coat pocket and lit it on the car lighter.

Now as he drove south toward Battery Park he could feel the cool comfort of the little 2-shot .38 palm gun gripped under the last two fingers of his right hand.

He drove the rental left-handed slowly down Seventh, resting his gun hand in his lap.

What's wrong with the money, Vesh Slovincik wondered. Why had James Lovell been late?

The lights of the theater district glinted brightly off the hood of the freshly waxed car. Beside him Lovell rattled the stones and made appreciative noises.

"Gem quality," he said aloud. "The Soviets' best."

Vesh heard the slur in Lovell's voice and wondered if the drunkenness was an act to make Vesh relax his guard. He took a deep breath and caught the strong smell of booze from the man's clothes.

Gin, Vesh decided. Martinis.

To his earlier list of questions Vesh added a new one: why does this Lovell need to have a few drinks before he comes to give me my money?

No answer he could think of felt good. Near the Port Authority Terminal Vesh turned right onto a side street.

"Where're we going?" Lovell asked in surprise. Vesh nodded to the right. There was nothing, but the financier turned anyway.

As he turned, Vesh pressed the palm gun to the back of his head and squeezed off a single round....

In the club bag Vesh found his delivery fee—$50,000 in crisp, green *counterfeit* bills. Lovell had tried to cheat him for the last time.

Theoretically, Vesh told himself, James Lovell was a good thief. The financier had fouled up the way a junkie fouls up. He couldn't take the strain of a crisis. He had to fortify himself first. Drugs or booze, Vesh thought as he pushed the body from the parked car, it's all the same.

He pulled away from the body unhurriedly and cruised eastbound on a one-way street in the direction of his hotel. The diamonds presented Vesh with an entirely new problem. Without Lovell's connection he had no idea how to unload them or how much they were worth.

Suddenly Vesh laughed at his worried face in the rearview mirror. It was nice to worry about having too much money for a change. As Vesh's laughter spilled out of the driver's window into the dark back streets of New York's garment district, an idea came to him. He knew exactly how to use the counterfeit money.

He'd sell it to the Russians for more diamonds.

That would be perfect, Vesh thought. James Lovell had already set up the second deal. The Soviet black marketeers were hungry for hard currency and the club bag contained $50,000 worth of good fakes.

I'll make one more trip, Vesh Slovincik promised himself. After that I'll retire.

WHAT HAD HAPPENED in Montreal?

The gaunt, seated figure pushed the plate of sliced fruit out of his way on the desk in front of him. He hunched forward in his chair and read the communiqué one more time.

Molinz dead.

Demeter—*Demeter*—also dead.

No one had seen the strike on the KGB's observation post, but Greb Strakhov recognized the style: a sudden, violent blitz by one man. It had to be Bolan.

A wave of something like fear washed over the general's scalp and left it tingling. What is this, he asked himself. Strakhov is getting soft?

His own disbelief at the unvoiced question reassured him. He stretched a large liver-spotted hand to the plate of fruit and picked up the discarded rind of a quartered lemon.

His scalp still tingled, but now it was with the violence of his own will.

Strakhov dropped the lemon rind into his mouth and smashed down on it with his back teeth.

Then he grinned.

I still have my teeth, the general thought. He ground the lemon peel to pulp, wishing it were Bolan. The sense of his own mortality that had struck him only moments ago was completely gone.

So he hunts me again, Strakhov decided. So what?

The general looked up from the cluttered desk in the KGB's New York safe house. The air in the room was cold. Strakhov could see traces of his own breath as he stared over the lamp toward the door.

The windows had been blacked out, but even so it was clear to him that evening had passed. It was now night.

And here I sit like an old man waiting for the Executioner to find me. Strakhov laughed. "Strassko!" he shouted at the door. He heard the booted feet crossing the hallway in the anteroom outside. A second voice was shouting for Strassko down the stairs.

The man performed well, Strakhov decided, thinking of Colonel Molinz's subordinate. He brought me the Japanese and the girl. He will be rewarded.

Greb Strakhov put on his most forbidding face as Sergei Strassko knocked and entered the dark room.

He did not return Strassko's salute. His hooded eyes scanned the younger man with the cold-bloodedness of a snake.

Strassko stood up to the scrutiny. Strakhov allowed himself to relax. He reclined in the chair, knowing that as he did so his face was hidden by shadows. It was an interrogator's trick and it was unintentional, merely a habit developed over the years of questioning prisoners and suspecting subordinates.

"You did well in Montreal."

Strassko's face clearly showed his surprise. Despite the emotionless tone of Strakhov's voice, Strassko had been complimented.

"Dr. Kanamuto will cooperate now," he volunteered. "It was only necessary to break a few of the girl's fingers."

The shadow of Strakhov's head moved on the hardwood floor. He was nodding at Strassko's good news. "Kill her," he said. "We don't need her anymore."

"We need to keep control of Kanamuto," Strassko objected.

"He'll believe what we tell him," Strakhov said offhandedly. "He's an old man. He needs his illusions. Kill her."

Strassko indicated his willingness.

"I want you to transport the doctor to Siberia," Strakhov told him. Again Strassko's face showed some surprise. That had been Molinz's job.

"Molinz and Demeter died in Montreal," Strakhov said.

Strassko's face registered concern. "How..." he began.

Strakhov caught something false in his tone. Strassko had heard it himself, even as he was saying it. Be more careful, he warned himself. Strakhov had brought his gaunt, predatory face out of the shadows and was searching Strassko's eyes.

The pale hooded eye sockets squinted at him questioningly. Strassko felt as if a searchlight had found him as he tried to escape across a border.

"Molinz *will* need a replacement," Strakhov said carefully.

He's testing me, Strassko thought. His face remained completely impassive. He said nothing, volunteered nothing.

Strakhov leaned back into the shadows. "You will replace Molinz," he said finally in a relaxed voice. Wisps of vapor flitted into the light.

Strassko's heart pounded, but his face wore the granite expression of the professional soldier. "Your orders, General?"

When Strakhov spoke again, the tension had subsided. "Transport the prisoner," he said, "to Vladivostok in the usual way. Supervise it personally and do it tonight." Strassko nodded.

"I will travel to China," Strakhov continued. "You will bring the prisoner to me there. Transport will be waiting when you reach Vladivostok.

"Aboard the transport, comrade," Strakhov added casually, "there will be an explosive device. Can you guess what it is for?"

Strassko nodded again but said nothing. After questioning the old Japanese man, the senior KGB agent had discovered a great deal about Strakhov's Chinese target, the bacteriological weapons testing site of the old Japanese Imperial Army.

When he gets the germs he wants, Strassko decided, the crazy old man is going to blow up the bug factory.

He couldn't see the general's face, but something convinced Strassko that Strakhov was grinning. The fact that he could not see those thin lips drawn back into what he knew would be a laughing death mask made his presence in the room take on a nightmarish quality. He felt drugged and vaguely dreamy.

It did not last long.

"Load the prisoner tonight," Strakhov snapped as though a new concern had reentered his thoughts and destroyed his good mood forever. Strassko turned to leave.

He could hear the general rise behind him and hastily begin scooping papers into his leather bag.

"Kill the girl," Strakhov repeated as Strassko closed the door. There was concern in the voice.

Strassko left the anteroom and headed for the basement cells. He meant to kill the girl immediately but suddenly the penny dropped. The brain of Molinz's replacement revved.

He knows it was Bolan in Montreal, Strassko thought.

Strakhov wants me to kill the girl *before* Bolan can get to her.

Just as quickly, another thought came to him. The Executioner is coming here tonight.

Strassko decided to load Dr. Kanamuto very quickly indeed. He made his way to the basement and examined the crate labeled Machine Parts in which Dr. Kanamuto would be transported to the USSR.

Overhead the outside door closed. No one had to tell Sergei Strassko that General Greb Strakhov had just left.

He is afraid of Bolan, Strassko thought suddenly. He was surprised at the audacity of his own mind.

Strakhov is weak, Strassko decided, and as it had in the General's office less than half an hour before, his heart began to pound.

I can exploit his weakness, Strassko thought. I can use Bolan to remove Strakhov.

Senior Agent Sergei Strassko had decided to move up in the ranks of the KGB again. Behind him he heard a moan from the cell holding Dr. Kanamuto's niece.

She is such a pretty flower, Strassko remembered. He had not liked breaking her fingers. It was a waste.

A new idea occurred to him. After ordering a guard to load Dr. Kanamuto, he entered the dark cell.

"Hello again, Reiko," he said to the woman shackled to the army cot.

She lifted her head hopefully, then shrank against the wall when she recognized her torturer.

"I am going to save you and your uncle," Strassko said soothingly as he approached her.

He ran his eyes along her body, savoring the fine, dark hair, the full breasts that seemed ready to fall out of the loose silk blouse.

He sat down beside her on the cot and touched her thigh. She recoiled from his touch. "You have to be nice to me now." Strassko smiled. "Let me tell you where I am taking your uncle..."

3

From behind the wheel of a rented van in East Brooklyn, Mack Bolan examined the location that the dead man had told him was a KGB safe house.

Was Strakhov in there?

Bolan doubted it. Security was too lax. Besides, he had spotted another set of watchers across the street from the safe house. They had to be CIA. Nobody else would be so interested in the doings of the KGB.

So Bolan thought.

If Strakhov was here, the Executioner reasoned, the CIA would have moved in by now.

Mack Bolan needed to know what was in that house.

Demeter had told him nothing but the location of Strakhov. Now Bolan was in the Russian community called Brighton Beach to capitalize on that hard-won piece of intel.

He watched the street again for activity, but there was only the occasional citizen going about his business. A walk to the liquor store, a leg stretch with the dog to avoid the missus. There was never much pedestrian traffic in this neighborhood at this time of night.

Bolan left the wheel and moved to the back of the van. If he wanted to get into the house he would have to take out the other watchers first. He knew he needed an edge to get close to what he thought was the CIA's van. Bolan pulled out the sandals and the robes. Soon he was in his disguise.

The man walking lightly down the street toward the parked van didn't look like the average Hare Krishna. He was too big, for one thing. Still, the robes fit him well enough and he looked empty and far away like a member of the chanting cult.

He stopped a middle-aged Russian man on his way home.

The old man dressed in worker's clothes was carrying a plastic grocer's sack that contained a few clinking bottles. He didn't look rich. Maybe he'd already had a few and was just feeling generous. It was Christmastime, after all. Maybe it was the Krishna's rap. Anyway, the old Russian bought the incense and wished the orange-clad figure a Merry Christmas. Mack Bolan smiled.

He pocketed the money and walked toward the back door of the van.

Inside he could hear foreign voices.

A puzzled expression crossed his face, but he didn't slow his pace. He pulled the auto-loading Magnum from an inside pocket of the orange ski jacket and opened wide both back doors to the van.

A man wearing headphones was seated at a surveillance console to Bolan's left.

He snapped his head around to face the Executioner. A hand went automatically toward the Smith and Wesson beside him.

"Don't," the Executioner said, but it was doubtful the man would have understood him, anyway.

He was Chinese. His reflexes had swung him into an action that he could not hope to win. The Oriental was fast, but not fast enough.

Behind this first man, a second tugged at an impressive piece of armament that Bolan immediately identified as a caseless H&K G-11.

But the pistol of the electronics man swung up in a broad arc.

"Don't, dammit!" Bolan said. The AutoMag thundered in the big guy's hand and blew the man's head apart. The second man was gore smeared and shaken. He twisted the H&K around to Bolan.

The Executioner blew him to hell.

The caseless gun clattered to the ground.

There was no turning back now. Bolan had intended to take down these watchers silently. He had wanted nothing more than the intel gathered from a soft probe into the safe house.

Now that was impossible.

The Soviets would be scrambling, and the superior firepower would surely help.

The Executioner picked up the G-11 and grabbed the plastic stack of magazines from behind the dead driver. Mack Bolan hoped with his entire being that Strakhov would be inside the house. He wanted April Rose to rest easily at last.

Was there a guard inside the door?

It no longer seemed important. The wood came away effortlessly. It collapsed inward with a short snap from the heel of Bolan's boot.

He was already firing the G-11—Demeter *had* told him that there would be at least four men inside. One, a guard, was peering through the hall window to his left as the Executioner entered.

Bolan shredded him with a flurry of fire from the assault weapon. He knew from his career as a jungle fighter that he had exactly the right weapon in his hands.

Each G-11 bullet, the Executioner recalled, was set into a solid block of propellant and required no empty shell to be cleared. As a result, the incredible rate of fire was two thousand rounds a minute.

Bolan caught a glimpse of a man's shadow moving through a door at the end of a dark hallway. He switched the death system to floating fire and the H&K spewed its pinpoint shells in a wave pattern up and down the wall separating both men.

Bolan heard a ragged scream of horror and surprise. He fired again and was satisfied to hear the solid bump of a body striking hardwood.

Plasterboard walls, Bolan reflected, offered very little resistance to this remarkable weapon.

In the lull, Bolan grabbed for the plastic sack and loaded another hundred rounds.

Since he had entered the house, The Executioner had barely come halfway down the front hall. Now he heard booted feet running for the stairwell.

No problem, thought the man. He swept the weapon almost casually in an arc across the ceiling. Someone spilled down the staircase beside him. He was alive but his limbs jerked out of control.

Bolan allowed the man a short mercy burst, then turned again to the doorway at the end of the long hall. There was at least one man left.

Bolan dearly hoped it was Strakhov.

A voice from the kitchen shouted, "Surrender! I surrender!" First in good English, then in Russian.

A pistol came skidding down the hallway floor but Bolan was unconvinced. "Show yourself!" he shouted.

The man at the far end had been waiting just for that. He had a fix on the Executioner's voice and would have killed him if Bolan had not moved when he spoke.

The man came through the kitchen door, emptying a Scorpion into the spot Bolan had occupied seconds before. When he looked up, the Executioner was beside him with the thin mouth of the G-11 pointed directly at the man's eye.

He meant to question him but the terrified man reacted with his nerves and not his brain. Bolan made a mess of him and then checked the kitchen.

It was empty. An open door led to the basement, but he decided that could wait. He was on the kill now for Strakhov.

An idea occurred to him. He opened the refrigerator door and was rewarded with an abundance of food. Yes, there were lemons. He smelled one. It was a Caucasus. Strakhov might still be here!

Bolan let the full force of his hate for the man wash over him.

In such moments he felt himself to be not just a physical body moving from place to place by means of muscle and tissue and bone.

In such moments when the promise of Strakhov's death was before him, Mack Bolan felt at last that he was made of pure energy.

The Executioner left the kitchen and flooded through the house, entering and filling every room as if he were a blazing flame of colored light.

In the office on the second floor he found an empty desk with a plate of half-eaten lemons and the blaze went cold. The lemons were like the bitterness of the Executioner's hunt.

Once more Strakhov had eluded him....

In the basement Mack Bolan found the girl's cell.

He had to shoot the door to get to her, and her screams filled the house. She was terrified. As soon as he entered the cell he saw why.

"Easy, honey. I'm not going to hurt you." She continued screaming, and Bolan crossed the cell quickly. He didn't want to, but he clapped his hand over her mouth to silence her. It had the expected effect. She began struggling.

Bolan caught both her wrists in one hand and held her.

He said soothing things to her till she quieted. Then he took his hand away from her mouth.

"Who did this to you?" he asked.

"He said his name was Strakhov," the girl sobbed.

Bolan kept his disbelief from showing on his face. Strakhov was evil. Bolan, of all men, knew that. But he also knew the KGB chief didn't rape helpless girls, at least not out of any need for sexual violence. The only passion Greb Strakhov knew was the passion of hatred, pure and simple.

"He took my uncle," the young woman wailed.

"Where?" Bolan demanded.

"Vladivostok," she said.

"Why?" Bolan asked, genuinely surprised. Before she could answer Bolan heard boots on the stairs. He dropped the woman's hand and seized his assault rifle.

From the doorway he could see three Orientals crouching beside the basement stairs. They were all armed. The weapons were Ingrams.

A woman's voice came from somewhere off to the side. He stretched toward it but still could not see its source. "We demand that you surrender Dr. Kanamuto," the woman said.

"Is the doctor a woman?" Bolan asked.

"The doctor," the voice replied icily, "is a very old man."

"Then you're barking up the wrong tree, dolly," Bolan shot back. "There's just me and a girl in here."

"How can we be sure?" the woman asked.

Bolan chuckled. "Easiest thing in the world. You just walk right through my gunsights and come in here to check."

After a long pause the woman spoke again. "I will do exactly that," she said. Bolan heard a body in motion, the rustling of a garment brushing against moving legs. One of the three gunmen apparently protested in a singsong sentence that could have meant "Don't be an idiot." The woman with the voice silenced him with a short phrase whose meaning was equally clear.

Bolan backed away from the door, expecting trouble. It could easily have been a dodge, a way of distracting him, then rushing the cell.

They'd have to want the doctor very badly for that, Bolan thought. Or they'd have to be blind when they walked through the destruction he'd left on the upper floors.

It wasn't a trick. The woman came through the door coolly and unarmed. She, too, was Chinese.

She gave Bolan the most disdainful look he'd ever received from a woman. She scanned the cell and looked interestedly at the prisoner.

"Dr. Kanamuto's niece," she said to no one. She looked directly at Bolan then.

"You didn't rape her," she said. "You didn't have time."

Mack Bolan didn't know how this intruder had gotten under his skin so easily and he didn't care. He slapped her before she could speak again, and she stepped back from him, stunned.

"Take your playmates and get out," Bolan told her. She backed toward the cell door unnecessarily. The Executioner had already turned away from her. He was removing the shackles from Dr. Kanamuto's niece.

Behind him he heard the clatter of the Chinese hardguys on the stairs. They might try to kill us when we leave here, the Executioner thought. On reconsideration, he decided they'd had enough for one day.

He shook the thoughts of the second woman from his head as he hefted Dr. Kanamuto's niece in his arms. He noticed that her thumbs had been broken. She must be in intense pain, Bolan thought. He was glad he hadn't wasted more time questioning that princess.

Anyway, something inside him said that silk skirt would be turning up again. The Executioner wasn't looking forward to it.

4

"Okay, Reiko," Mack Bolan said to the pretty woman in the hospital bed. "You just tell it to this man the way you told it to me...." Hal Brognola listened intently as the young woman recounted the story of her ordeal.

Brognola interrupted her frequently. At one point he left the room for more than an hour while he "made some calls."

Brognola returned to the room grim-faced and nodded for Bolan to come outside with him. "I've put a guard in the hall, Miss Kanamuto," Brognola told the girl. "You're fine now. You're a very lucky woman...."

"Please save my uncle," she begged. Her appeal was directed to Bolan. He gave her a smile and stepped into the hallway with Brognola.

"What have you got, Hal?" the Executioner wondered. He had had no contact with the Fed since Brognola had tipped him about Molinz's presence in Montreal. They had some ground to cover.

"Reiko Kanamuto's been straight with us, Mack," Brognola said, offering his friend a Marlboro. He lit one himself and glanced down the empty hall.

"Trouble is, she doesn't know anything about her uncle."

"Dr. Kanamuto."

"Right. At least he's some kind of doctor. Butcher would be a better word."

Bolan waited for it.

"He was a reasearch scientist in China during World War II," Brognola said. "The Japanese had a testing facility in the northeast. A place called Harbin."

"I've heard of it. What kind of research?"

"Bugs." Bolan looked puzzled, so Hal continued. "Germs. Bacteria. Viruses. You name it. They cooked up some pretty scary stuff before they surrendered."

"So why is he a butcher?" Bolan demanded.

"Get this, Mack, the Japanese used human subjects. They developed strains of viruses that would only attack the indigenous populations of their enemies."

"What's that mean?"

"They had bugs that would cause disease to the Chinese but not to the Japanese. The biology of each race is minutely but significantly different, and they capitalized on that. The same goes for the Soviets *and*—" Hal paused for effect "—the same for us. Kanamuto himself was in charge of the Chinese and American research."

"Where'd he get Americans?"

"POWs and missionaries."

"How many are we talking about?" Bolan asked.

"Don't ask," Brognola told him. "It just makes me sick. Thing is, the Japanese surrendered to the Americans, and Kanamuto and the rest of this mob traded their bugs for immunity. That's why he's walking around today." Brognola had forgotten about the cigarette in his fingers. He tossed it to the floor suddenly and stomped on it with disgust. It might have been a bug.

Bolan waited until a nurse passed. "How does Strakhov figure in it?" he asked.

Brognola heaved a big breath, definitely not a sigh. "The story goes that the bug research was carried out at an underground site. A storage bunker with natural ice caves, that kind of thing. The story also goes that the bugs Kanamuto gave us were nothing on what's still stashed in the ice caves."

"And Strakhov...?"

"With one or two vials from Kanamuto's secret stash, our good general could become the most powerful figure in the Soviet Union. These are superbugs, Mack. You just can't defend yourself against a weapon that's this invisible and this selective."

"So I find Kanamuto," Bolan thought out loud. "Then I find the bugs and destroy them. Then I kill Strakhov."

"Yeah. Dead simple." Brognola grinned tiredly at his friend's determined face. "I can help you some, Mack. We've got a fix on Kanamuto. At least we think we do."

"Come on, Hal." Bolan's anger showed. "Give."

"They *may*—I'm using that advisedly, Mack—they may be taking him out in a box of machine parts bound for Siberia. It was loaded onto a freighter a few hours before you did your song and dance in Brooklyn. There's more." Now Hal was grinning.

"INS picked up a sailor when that freighter first came in. He was smuggling a handful of diamonds. Anyway, they need crew. Your papers'll be waiting for you at the pier."

Now Bolan too was grinning. "Thanks, Hal."

"There's something more, Mack."

Bolan turned back toward the Fed questioningly. "We want the bugs, Mack. Especially if the Russians have got 'em. This comes from very high up. The best case is we get the bugs and nobody else does."

"I don't like it, Hal. I won't do it."

"Yeah." Brognola grinned again. "I can't order you to."

"No, you can't."

"Okay. Look, off the record, Mack, these things are bad news for everybody." Bolan understood.

What he didn't understand was how Strakhov had come to operate with such a free hand inside China. Hal had no thoughts but admitted it was "fishier than hell."

Bolan turned away from the Fed to leave, and Brognola caught his arm. "Don't you think you'd better change, Mack?" he asked, smirking.

Bolan accepted a satchel of clothes. He was still wearing the ski jacket and the orange robe. "Guess I look conspicuous, huh?"

THE AMERICAN WAS IN THE GALLEY KITCHEN feeling the freighter lurch again as it took the blow of yet another wave amidships. His coffee slopped out of the hot cup in his hand and splashed steaming across the surface of the table and onto the floor. It was his third cup and he had yet to finish one of them.

He rubbed the back of his scalded right hand and went for a refill. He knew he would need the stimulant to stay awake during the coming four-hour shift.

The galley was empty and lit by fluorescent bulbs in wire cages. Their putrid light accentuated the lateness and the loneliness and the danger of the storm.

He had pulled the graveyard again, because he had the least seniority of the crew. His forged seafarer's card gave him less time in than any other man aboard. Also, the man he replaced, Manfeld, had been the *Tito I*'s odd-jobber.

Times like these he dreaded most; the stillness and quiet left him alone with himself. Times that used to be for making sense of things when the world was coming apart.

Now, instead of making sense in his loneliness he was pla-
gued by the cruel and insistent voices of despair that he
could not drown out.

The light stared at him from behind its cage. April
Rose's death was incomprehensible to him.

Mack still fought for everything he believed in. Just as
surely as he walked the hellgrounds. Only now he could
not stand the stillness. He needed the action just to keep
himself going.

He could not slow down without crashing, always coming up against one thing: April's death. Why did she have
to die, he asked for the thousandth time. All his philoso-
phy and certainty of knowledge slipped off in the wind
when he thought of her death, leaving him desolate and
mute.

To live we must love. Mack never forgot that it was the
ultimate purpose, the only thing that enabled human
beings to rise above their brutality and ugliness. Mack of
all people knew that without love there was only hate.

Mack had lost his love. Hate was slowly filling the empty
space he had reserved especially for her. Now he walked
the hellgrounds fighting not only the evil manifest in men,
but the ghosts of his own pain, as well.

From the sudden pitch of the ship he knew another big
wave was going to break over him. This time he placed a
saucer over the coffee mug. His body rolled forward and
snapped back in his chair but he kept his left hand securely fastened to the top of the mug.

When the ship settled he took out his smokes and lit up.
How long before he becomes one of the hateful, filling a
senseless life with senseless violence? And would he know
it when he crossed that line?

UP ON THE BRIDGE, the night was a frigid version of hell.

In this inferno waves replaced flames, and the only tormented souls for thousands of hectares were those aboard the *Tito I*.

The Yugoslav freighter was loaded with a shipment of American grain intended to supplement a year of bad Soviet harvests. Its holds were laden. An experienced sailor might have said overladen, considering the conditions of this sea.

Despite the weight of the grain, however, there was one hold that was almost empty. The manifest had said it contained machine parts, but Vesh Slovincik had only seen one crate being lowered into it.

That had aroused his curiosity. But when he returned at night to check it out he found the hold sealed. The seal was standard Border Police. Vesh stole a couple from the captain's desk and returned the next night.

He had been thinking that a sealed hold would be a perfect place to hide his American currency.

Inside the hold he encountered only one crate, the same one he had helped load. It was tethered to the bulkhead in a sloppy way. The Yugoslav could tell that the man who'd done it was no sailor.

There was a passenger on this trip. A military looking type who kept to his cabin. Vesh had heard him inside throwing up when the sea got rough.

This would be his work.

He wondered about the connection between the crate and the passenger but decided that he didn't need to know. Something in the hold stank of politics, and as a citizen under a Communist regime, Vesh Slovincik knew that politics was nothing to get involved with.

So he stashed his American dollars in the hold, resealed it and went about his business.

Tonight as he took the watch Vesh's thoughts went to the crate in the sealed hold. Ordinarily he liked the night watch. Ordinarily rough seas were only that to him, rough seas.

He had seen the worst that any ocean had to offer, or so he thought. But it was bad tonight. Bad because of the weight of the cargo and the creaking, brittle age of the vessel herself.

When his mind drifted back to the crate labeled Machine Parts, Vesh wondered how fragile those parts could be.

In a storm like this one, he knew that the rope job on the crate would give way. He was wondering if he should take his money from the sealed hold before someone decided to check out the crate.

Another massive breaker crashed across the deck, and Vesh decided to stay on the bridge. It was suicide to go out into the night. The money would just have to take care of itself.

One thing was certain—nobody else would be visiting the sealed hold tonight.

As the breaker crashed, Vesh's large hands automatically caught the console before him. He lurched from starboard to port and felt his shoulders snap back to starboard again as the ship steadied.

Vesh scanned the deck for damage, but the soupy water that washed over the bridge obscured his vision. The water cleared the window like the paw of some sea beast.

Vesh could imagine the sea beast aiming lazy blows at the *Tito I*'s deck. Each casual blow landed with the force of an earthquake.

The port cleared. No damage.

He checked his instruments and glanced at the clock. It was 0340, and his relief was due at 0400. Vesh wondered how many more breakers could tag the ship in twenty minutes. It was a good game to play. A good way to pass time.

Vesh loved to count.

He especially loved to count money. Tonight, however, waves would have to do.

He noticed that the big ones came in on every ninth wave. He watched the wire-caged ship's clock timing the breakers to see if they were evenly spaced.

By the time the ninth wave hit, they were averaging fifty-three seconds apart.

When everything is working right, the sailor thought, the world runs like a good watch. He was timing the ninth wave when it broke. His eyes were on the clock. The wave was more than half a minute late. It was huge.

As Vesh looked up, he saw it come in. Its giant gaping maw was gray caped, and the caps looked like teeth that could easily devour the old *Tito I*.

Vesh thought the wave looked like a Florida gator snapping into a brittle bone. He had seen that in zoos. At the time he had felt pretty much like the gator. Now he felt like the bone.

The jaws snapped. Vesh was driven to the floor. The old brass fittings on the starboard entrance to the bridge burst with the wave's force.

That breaker must be eighty-five or ninety feet, Vesh thought.

His hands caught the leg of the console and he held on. Water rushed through the bridge and returned, lapping over the door frame. Gallons remained and washed back to Vesh's position on the floor. It soaked him a second time.

The brine was like ice.

The ship steadied and Vesh stood up, swearing in hill-country dialect that sounded like a family of goats chewing tin cans and breaking wind.

He slammed the door shut, but the force of his push and the wind outside caused it to bounce back.

Cursing, Vesh noticed the broken fittings. The breaker had sheared the brass lock and left a twisted chunk of metal dangling midway up the door.

In his anger, Vesh tore it away.

He was cold and wet. The brief contact with the seawater had chilled him to the bone. From the locker behind the wheel he grabbed a slicker and put it on.

Wind from the door tugged at the heavy fabric and made it a chore to fasten the slicker's front. He turned away and fastened the garment.

Got to jam that door, he thought.

Then the big wave broke.

Water burst through the open cabin door behind Vesh Slovincik like a jet cleansing the bowl of an enormous flush toilet.

Vesh had just looked up from the slicker. He saw the wave behind his back reflected in the port-side window. He also saw a terrified man, a man he didn't recognize, a man dressed in a slicker like the one he had on.

The wave was filling the cabin, crashing into the reflected man's back, sweeping him in a collision course with Vesh.

Vesh realized he was the reflected man. He had not recognized the mirror image of the face that was distorted by terror.

Both of the sailor's faces collided. The impact shattered the tempered glass and the sailor fell.

Under the icy water that filled the cabin the Yugoslav's mind snapped back into alert. The backwash dragged him across the cabin toward the door, toward the open sea. It was happening fast, but Vesh fought the violence every centimeter.

The water was an irresistible force but he flailed his arms, grabbing anything that obstructed them. This time his grip on the console was not strong enough to resist the force of the backwash and the starboard lurch of the ship.

He tumbled through the cabin. The door loomed. He spread his arms. He made his body into a cross. His hand held him momentarily at the threshold.

Outside the sea was a caldron.

The ship lurched again. Vesh was thrown through the door, crushed against the railing by the weight of the icy water behind him. He grabbed for the railing.

Will I hold? Will I hold? His body was a question mark. Everything was in suspension.

The water behind him flipped him over the rails. He dangled backward under the bridge, feeling the ice grow in his fingers and the last of the water from the bridge hammer at him as it left the rails.

I'm done, Vesh Slovincik thought.

He hung backward, counting the seconds to the next big wave....

The American finished his coffee and butted the smoke. The cigarette had been stale and had given him little enjoyment. It was still early, but he decided to go to the bridge. When he popped the door from the galley, the floor was awash with seawater.

Mack Bolan began to move very fast....

There was no feeling in Vesh's right hand and very little in his left. He honestly did not know what was holding him on to the railing. I must be frozen to it, he thought.

Death was just a few seconds away now, and Vesh was doing everything to keep it out of his mind. He had tried

praying. Images of James Lovell's lifeless body had filled
his brain, but still he prayed. He promised God anything.
It was the dying prayer of a frightened hypocrite. Even
Vesh knew that.

His forearms were frozen now, so at first he did not feel
the American's hands gripping his wrists. But there was
something, something above the roar of the sea.

He looked straight over the rail. Someone was standing
above him. He was backward, so Vesh couldn't make out
the face. Someone was gripping his wrists and shouting.

"Let go, dammit! I've got to pull you up!"

"FRO-ZEN!" he shouted. He realized that the ninth
wave was coming very soon, but he didn't warn the man.
Vesh Slovincik was greedy to live. If it cost the guy above
him his life, well, that was his lookout.

The American drove the extended fingers of his right
hand into Vesh's left. It was a good guess that the dangling man was right handed. The hand released, but the big
man gripped it in his own. He held Vesh's right hand in his
left and pivoted the dangling sailor so that he faced the
bridge.

Vesh could feel the wave building behind him, but with
the change in his position accomplished he felt renewed
hope. His legs worked frantically, trying to get a purchase
on the slippery bulkhead below the railing. They were cold,
cold as his hands, but the muscle groups were larger and
Vesh knew it was his last chance. His legs moved. They had
to.

It was futile work. There were no footholds on the side
of the bridge. The wave was building behind him and still
Vesh did not shout a warning at his rescuer.

It seemed now to the sailor that the big man above him
had simply begun to pull him up by the wrists.

He'll never do it, Vesh thought, mindful of his ninety-eight-kilo body weight. He'll never do it.

The American's shoulders flexed. He drew the Yugoslav straight up in the air until the man's torso hung over the railing. Then he flipped him head down and dragged his feet over.

With only seconds left before the big wave broke, Vesh struggled to his feet. He pushed his rescuer aside with a desperate shove of his right arm and dived into the bridge.

He would have slammed the bridge door on the Executioner but the American was much faster than the desperate, flabby coward.

Bolan hurled his shoulder into it and sent the sailor flying. "The wave!" Slovincik shouted in Russian.

Bolan sneered at the man's fear and pulled a metal locker to the floor to jam the door closed.

The wave struck. The locker didn't keep the door closed, but it did keep both men inside. There was only a foot of water on the bridge deck this time, but Mack Bolan ignored it.

He was giving Vesh Slovincik the worst beating of his life.

Slovincik was slow to respond at first. Bolan hit him backhand and sent him against the window he had broken earlier.

When the sailor fell, the Executioner kicked him, hard, in his butt. The man groaned and tried to stand. Mack Bolan drove his fist into the back of his neck.

Vesh collapsed again in the icy water. Bolan could see the man's hand fumbling under the water where his right boot should have been. The Executioner reached under his wet coat and withdrew the AutoMag.

"If there's a weapon in your hand I'm going to kill you," he said.

The idea of having a gun pulled on him by a man he had just rescued was too much for Mack Bolan. He wished now that he'd let the sea take this one. The man was a gutless snake.

It was not too late, Bolan thought, staring at the defeated sailor's face. Vesh must have read the Executioner's mind. "Let me live, American," he said.

"I need a reason," Bolan told him.

"Fifty thousand dollars," the man said. "It's yours. Let me live."

Bolan snorted. "You're a merchant seaman. You've never seen $50,000."

"I have it, I swear," Vesh told him. "It's in the empty hold."

Bolan's attention increased. Kanamuto's crate had to be in that hold.

"You can't get in there," Bolan countered. "It's sealed."

"I've got a seal," Vesh told him. "I've got $50,000 American *and* I've got a seal."

"What've you got in your boot?" Bolan wondered.

"Palm gun," the man told him. "Two shots. That's all."

"Make sure it stays there," Bolan said. He gestured with the AutoMag, and the Yugoslav stood up out of the water.

"Where are we going?"

"To visit a war criminal," Bolan told him.

KANAMUTO WAS DEAD.

Bolan knew it as soon as he saw the crate. It had torn loose from its ropes and was lying on its side in the hull of the heaving boat.

"Here is the money," Vesh said. The sailor was standing behind the Executioner as he examined the falling crate. His thoughts were on the gun in his boot.

"Don't try it," Bolan told him. Vesh was amazed. He had thought it too dark in the hold to see anything at the distance that separated them. He moved toward the Executioner.

The man was not looking at him. Instead Bolan was examining the top of the crate, which now lay on its side.

"Come over here," Bolan commanded. Vesh obeyed.

With a gesture, Bolan instructed the sailor to open the crate from the top. Vesh did so, using his clasp knife. Inside, Dr. Kanamuto's lifeless form stared up at them. His mouth was open and his eyes bulged.

He looked as though he had been born without a neck.

Bolan thought of Demeter. The Soviet agent had maintained his dignity and faced his death faultlessly. The Yugoslav sailor now turned away from the sickening sight of Kanamuto.

As he did so he caught Mack Bolan's eye. The Executioner couldn't help comparing Vesh Slovincik to the man he had known only as Demeter. Vesh Slovincik didn't measure up.

No way.

Bolan wondered what to do about Vesh. He couldn't put himself in the position of trusting something like Vesh. On the other hand, the killing time had passed.

Suddenly the Executioner smiled. "You say you saw this crate *before* we came here tonight?" Vesh nodded.

"Do you remember how it was secured?"

"Sure I remember. It was sloppy. That one knows nothing about knots."

Bolan nodded at the reference to the passenger. "Show me how it was," he said.

Vesh righted the crate and tied it. "You want me to put the lid back on?" he asked when he had finished.

"Not quite yet," Mack Bolan said as he zapped the sailor with the barrel of the Magnum. There was an extra length of cord in a corner and Bolan used it to truss Vesh.

He inserted the sailor in the crate and tied him up so that he was resting on Dr. Kanamuto's lap. I'd love to see Strakhov's face when he opens this, Mack Bolan thought to himself as he refastened the lid.

He picked up the fifty grand on his way out and re-sealed the hold in the way Vesh had showed him. The sea was not entirely calm, but the worst of the storm had passed. Bolan glanced at his watch.

The Executioner returned along the deck. When he reached the bridge he checked the bag holding the cur-rency. He was not too surprised that the money was coun-terfeit, but his disgust with Vesh Slovincik had reached a new low.

Mack Bolan tossed the money into the sea and picked up the mike to the intercom. "Canute!" he shouted to the man on duty in the radio room. "Man overboard!" He was just a little sorry that it wasn't true.

5

Mun Giyang was beautiful, but she was not a retiring Oriental flower. The thought that her father had agreed to cooperate with the Russians sickened her. She had never seen Strakhov, but at her father's insistence she had read the general's file.

What she read simply confirmed her impressions of all Westerners. Like the man who had slapped her in New York, Strakhov was *kwai lo*, a big-nosed barbarian. They only needed him now because she had not been able to reach Dr. Kanamuto in time.

Strakhov had been able to find Kanamuto first. That meant he had been able to learn the location of the viruses. Despite her protests, Mun's father, Ling, explained that the Chinese security police could not guard the Harbin ice caves indefinitely.

The caves were vast. No one knew how many entrances there were. Chinese geologists suspected the caves lay under the entire group of hills to the east of Harbin. Ling told her that the Soviets were certain to steal the germs if the Chinese did not agree to share them.

"These things should really be destroyed," he told her. "But if the Soviets have them, we *must* have them, too."

"The Soviets don't have them yet," Mun snapped.

Ling's face remained impassive. He knew his daughter's moods. I clung to her too closely after her mother died, he thought. I spoiled her.

"You are feeling bad because you failed to find Kanamuto in time," Ling said, smiling.

Mun's blush was one of anger, not shame. Her father had always been able to see through her. It was times like these that she hated him. He made her feel weak.

She hated that.

"How can the Soviets steal the germs from under your nose?" she asked. "If you refuse to cooperate, you close the door on them."

With a sad face, the director of Chinese Internal Security shook his head. "The KGB has an extensive network in China. You know this already," Ling said. "Once they have the location of Kanamuto's secret vault, nothing, *nothing*," he repeated, "will prevent them from recovering the germs."

"Then destroy them," Mun demanded.

At this suggestion Ling paused. He seemed to consider it.

"The geologist Shu told me the entire complex of caves rests over a small deposit of natural gas," Mun pressed. "If you create a big enough explosion at a low point in the cave, the gas will set up a chain reaction, a..."

"Fastburn," Ling supplied.

"Then you know?" Mum said, surprised. "The germs will burn up."

"I have spoken with the geologist Shu," Ling told her.

"Then it's settled," Mun said.

"Settled? No."

"Father," Mun insisted, "we can end this now. These things are *evil*." Ling smiled at the young woman's conviction. "They are *tainted*, Father. If we have them, it will bring suffering on us. And," she added vehemently, "if we deal with pig *kwai lo* they will double-cross us. We will be left with empty hands."

"If we use the fastburn solution," Ling told her, "we put the entire city of Harbin in danger."

Mun raised her head and looked down at him archly. Just like her mother, Ling thought. That woman had a gift for putting you in your place.

"That's just not true," Mun said. She left her chair in Ling's austere office and moved toward the door. Ling's eyes did not follow her, but his ears did. There was a rustle of silk against a moving leg that took him back twenty years.

Ling's wife, a university teacher, had died in the riots of the Cultural Revolution. Ling himself had spent fifteen years in a reeducation camp, waiting to die, until China's leaders decided he was a valuable man.

We were betrayed by our leaders then, Ling thought as Mun approached the door. Am I being betrayed now?

Mun's voice took him out of his reverie. "I have brought the geologist Shu with me," she said. "Talk to him. He will convince you that the fastburn option endangers no one."

Ling looked at his beautiful, angry daughter and came to a decision. "I know fastburn is harmless," he said. "I have read Shu's report."

"Then why...?" Mun nearly whined.

Ling stopped her with a gesture. "The secretary himself," he told the young woman, "has decided China must have these weapons."

Mun was visibly shocked.

"We have very little in our arsenal," Ling continued. "The Soviets have five armored divisions constantly posed on our northwestern border...."

"The army..." Mun countered.

"Is a national disgrace," Ling snapped. "If we are invaded we would have to use atomic weapons immediately, and we have barely a dozen of those. With one ground strike, the Soviet Union could set industrialization back *twenty years*!"

The Chinese spy master realized he was shouting. He lowered himself into his chair.

"The Soviets will never give you weapons that you can turn against them," Mun said flatly. Ling heard the truth in her words and nodded.

"I am aware of that," he told his daughter. "But until I have proof of their intention to cheat us, I can't disobey the secretary's order."

"What if I find the germs first?" Mun asked him.

"Please do it," Ling smiled. "That would change everything."

"I would rather see them destroyed," Mun told him.

So would I, Ling thought. "Strakhov will arrive in China tomorrow," he told her. "Find me the germs and I'll stop him at the frontier...." It was impossible, but Mun looked determined.

It pained the old spy to know that he was just encouraging his daughter in her vain hopes.

TECHNICALLY MACK BOLAN WAS on shore leave, but he hung around the deck of the moored freighter as the Soviet longshoremen off-loaded her.

It was the first time he'd seen Strassko.

The Executioner did not know the man's name but he knew he was the Russian who had remained sick and cabin bound throughout the voyage.

Bolan realized Strassko was the man who had raped Reiko Kanamuto. Her description had been very precise.

The business of Reiko could wait, however. Now Bolan was concerned with the destination of the crate labeled Machine Parts. Bolan knew that wherever Kanamuto went, Strakhov would be waiting.

Bolan turned his face away as Sergei Strassko brushed past. He had never before seen him, only knew of him through Kanamuto's description. The man obviously floated near the top of the KGB sewer. Bolan's photograph was a commonplace in Strakhov's Thirteenth Directorate.

Strassko tore the seal from the entrance to the empty hold as the Executioner watched from a distance.

The man turned back toward him once, but Bolan had a few weeks' growth on his face, which he was idly rubbing with a massive gloved hand. Whenever Strassko turned in his direction, he breathed out and the white cloud from his lungs obscured his face even more in the hard Siberian air.

But Strassko wasn't paying any attention to Bolan. He was shouting to the longshoremen in the hold. Anxious about his cargo, Strassko entered the hold while the other men were preoccupied.

Bolan sidled past, watching from the deck as Strassko knocked on the side of the crate.

There was a return knock from inside the one marked Machine Parts, and Bolan nearly laughed.

Nearly but not quite.

He imagined Strassko thinking that Kanamuto had returned his knock.

The longshoremen in the hold busied themselves fitting the outsize crate into the webbing. The foreman whistled up to the ship's crane when the webbing was secure. Kanamuto's body and Vesh Slovincik lurched free from the bowels of the *Tito I.*

Bolan stood to the far side of the hold, watching the crane lift the crate free of the opening. It was an easy task. The ship's crane was equipped to handle loads twenty times the weight of this crate.

Maybe it was too easy. The crane operator must have been used to the sluggish response of heavier burdens. He whisked the machine parts skyward with enough speed to launch them into orbit.

Bolan found this part funny, too. He knew the sailor inside wouldn't suffer from motion sickness but he *would* get one hell of a surprise. Yeah. It was funny, all right.

Funny until the webbing hit the side of the hold.

When that happened, the Executioner came on full alert. He cursed himself silently for relaxing. One of the four ropes binding the webbing to the crane's hook had sheared off from the contact with the metal bulkhead. The crate was in danger of spilling back into the hold and shattering.

If Strassko found Vesh Slovincik inside that crate, the Executioner would never get to the germs *or* Strakhov.

Mack Bolan glanced into the hold to where the foreman was making his way toward the deck. The man was preoccupied. If anyone was going to do anything, it would have to be Bolan. Strassko was still deep in the ship beneath his feet. He could see nothing of the crane or Bolan.

The Executioner whistled up the crane operator as the crate edged toward the lax side of its webbing. The crane man continued lifting the hook, knowing that to stop now was to lose the crate.

Bolan raised both arms and directed the operator calmly. He motioned for the man to swing the crate toward his own position, and the crane operator responded until the sliding crate was nearly over the Executioner's head.

He motioned the man to bring it down, and the crate came down. It slid a bit more as it touched the deck in front of him, but there wasn't a scratch on it when it landed.

Bólan made a thumbs-up sign to the grinning operator and tied off the sheared rope. He whistled again and the hoist lifted its burden over the side to a waiting flatbed.

"Nice work," said a voice behind him.

Mack Bolan froze. He had never heard Strassko speak, so he could not tell if it was the KGB man simply by hearing his voice.

The Executioner turned slowly. His mind was on the Magnum under his arm inside the buttoned pea jacket.

The man behind him was the foreman. "Nice work," he said again.

This time Bolan smiled. "I'd buy you the first drink," the foreman said, referring to the etiquette of Russian drinking habits, "but we have to take this thing to the airport."

An idea came into Bolan's mind in a hurry. "I'm headed that way myself," he said in a good Georgian accent. The Executioner had no trouble speaking everyday Russian. When things were simple, his accent was as good as the next man's.

"I'm outbound for Irkutsk, tonight," Bolan continued. "Can you give me a ride?"

"Sure," the foreman agreed. "It's easy. Give us a hand unloading the truck and *then* I'll buy the first drink."

They left the ship before Strassko emerged from the hold. From the foreman Bolan learned the KGB man would follow in an ancient Skaldia.

"Goroslov is in charge of the motor pool." The foreman laughed as he took the wheel of the Volga flatbed. "Goroslov hates KGB." He spat out the driver's window.

"That one—" he jerked his finger back toward the *Tito I* "—the one in the hold? You saw. Sure! He is KGB for sure!" The Executioner did his best to look surprised.

"Anyway, Goroslov knows that the car is for big-time, visiting KGB. He gives him a Skaldia! Ha!" The foreman's laughter filled the cab of the small truck. The man between Bolan and the foreman laughed, too.

"This ancient Skaldia," the second man said, "Goroslov calls it the Peace Talks." The foreman broke out in another gust of laughter. "Peace Talks," Bolan knew, was Russian for Disarmament Talks.

"You know why Goroslov calls it 'Peace Talks'?" the second man asked laughingly.

The foreman could not wait for the Executioner's answer. "It is always breaking down!" he roared. The three men were still laughing when they cleared customs.

The flatbed Volga pulled out of the shipyard toward the airport. With a little luck, the Executioner thought, I should be able to stow away on Kanamuto's plane.

WITH THE LANDSCAPE WHEELING and banking below, Mun searched the lower portion of the helicopter's canopy as her pilot banked right over the old Japanese Imperial Testing Facility. All that was left there was rubble. Kanamuto himself had issued the order to blow it up before surrendering to the Americans.

Mun Giyang knew why.

Kanamuto had wanted to cover his tracks. When he blew up the testing facility, he had blown up the evidence of his war crimes. Mun shuddered at the thought of them.

They were as horrible as anything the Nazis had ever attempted in Germany. And, for Mun Giyang, they were much closer to the heart.

Following Mun's instructions, the pilot banked and followed the ravine that cut across the grounds of the Japanese ruin. Mun had long suspected that the entrance Kanamuto had used to gain access to the caves had been very close to his facility.

There was no other explanation for its remaining a secret for all these years. True, she admitted to herself, the city was a good ten miles west but at the time there had been a large rural population. If the Japanese had been forced to transport the germs over a long distance on a regular basis, someone would have seen and remembered.

Mun Giyang smiled, realizing she had her father's gift for intelligence.

Beside her the pilot shouted, "Twenty minutes!" over the thump of the rotors. He was pointing at the fuel gauge. Mun nodded and gestured for him to continue down the right side of the ravine.

Beneath them the ground was covered with a thin layer of snow that had been coated with icy rain. The effect was like that of a painter's tarp drawn over the furniture of an entire room. The high points jutted under the white covering, and the low areas sagged.

Mun imagined she could see where the ground had been beaten into a road of some kind. When she had searched this place before, it had been high summer. There had been no road.

She shouted to the pilot, pointing to the spot they had just passed. He held them stationary and spun on the rotor, then headed back for the spot.

Suddenly Mun raised her hand.

The pilot hovered. Mun motioned down. The man lowered them slowly....

IT HAD BEEN A FEW HOURS since they had loaded Strakhov's machine parts on the empty transport plane. Strassko had still not shown up for takeoff.

Every thirty minutes the foreman, whose name Bolan discovered was Zom, would look at his watch and say, "Peace Talks." It was a good joke. The second man, Janus, laughed every time.

Bolan kept them company long enough to avoid suspicion. Finally he ducked out "to check on his flight to Irkutsk." When he left the Airport Workers' Club, he was already on the Vladivostok airstrip. He could see the transport waiting where they had loaded it. There were no guards. Only ground crew.

The KGB didn't need any guards in this place. The whole airport, Bolan decided, was an armed camp. He walked across the tarmac casually, keeping his face expressionless. That wasn't too hard.

Although it wasn't snowing, the wind on the open space at the airport was driving the beaded snow in misty, horizontal streaks over the curtain. The Executioner's face was screwed up like a prune as he pushed into the wind. No one could read his thoughts.

Even if they could, they would not be surprised. Mack Bolan had just made up his mind that Vladivostok was the coldest place on earth.

He had nothing but admiration for the ground crew who were working on the transport in the middle of this wind. An engineer working underneath the outside prop on Bolan's wing recognized him by his pea jacket and nodded.

Bolan said nothing. It wasn't necessary. No one could hear anything but the wind. Even the planes landed and took off in the buzzing, white storm of sound.

Bolan walked up the ramp in the belly of the plane. Inside it was like the belly of every other transport he'd ever been in. He heard the crew's voices in the cabin far ahead. He knew enough to avoid the men.

The front section of the transport was largely empty. Beside the ramp as he entered Bolan could see the Machine Parts crate, well secured this time, exactly where they'd left it.

There was a crated engine strapped to the floor amidships. This was the hiding place the Executioner had picked during his earlier reconnaissance. But first there was something he wanted to check.

There was a second wooden crate, about the size of a small fridge, near the one containing Kanamuto. Mack Bolan had had no time or privacy to examine it earlier, but it bore KGB markings and that made him *very* interested in its contents.

He slipped the pry bar he had taken from Zom's truck into a side of the crate and lifted the lid. The voices at the front of the aircraft maintained their conversational level. He focused his hearing on that level as he leaned inside the crate to check out the contents.

Bolan soon straightened, amazed, and very carefully replaced the carton's lid. He wanted to leave no trace on it. No suggestion it had been tampered with. He was sure that anyone who knew the contents would pay very close attention to it.

The Executioner had recognized the thing in the crate in an instant, despite the fact that he had only ever heard rumors of its existence....

6

The ice-covered surface of the snow underneath Mun's helicopter was the surest indication of the lay of the ground under the snow. Details of ground that were obscured by grass and scrub in the summer months were now exposed. It was as though the ice and snow were a large covering of stretch wrap. Every detail of what they covered showed to an airborne observer.

What Mun now saw was a bed of rubble where no rubble should be. The ravine at this point was a sheer surface of nearly vertical rock. But at one point, *this* point, there was a mound of debris at the base of the rock face.

I missed this last time, Mun thought. It would have easily been covered by the hom berries that flowered here all summer.

Now that she noticed the spot, Mun also noticed a slight gouge above it in the rock wall.

Kanamuto used explosives to destroy the testing facility, she remembered. That he had tried to hide the vault entrance in the same way seemed very likely to her.

Very likely.

Mun motioned for the pilot to land. "Fifteen minutes!" he protested, referring to the fuel.

Mun shot him her best look of disdain. The pilot glanced away and started the descent.

On the ground the snow lay deeper than Mun had expected. There was at least a foot of soft powder under brittle crust. Her feet sank into the powder with each loud step as she lurched toward the rubble. She could feel the eyes of the pilot on her.

She was certain the man was laughing at her! She turned back toward him and caught the simpleton grinning broadly.

"Get over here!" she shouted to him.

"I have no boots," he said, shrugging.

"Get over here!" It was an order. She was still the man's cadre. She was damned if she would let him laugh at her.

The pilot's grin was replaced by a look of disgust. He started toward her.

"Wait!" Mun shouted. "Bring something we can dig with."

"There is nothing!" the pilot shouted to her.

"Bring your gun," she said.

The man pretended not to hear her. He continued moving toward her in the snow, picking his way gingerly in his People's Liberation Army sneakers.

"The gun!" Mun insisted.

The pilot snarled, but he turned back for it. Damn that woman, he thought. If not for her father, someone would have stopped her train a long time ago. She was worse than the roving packs of wolves, the reason he kept the gun in his chopper in the first place.

Now she wanted to dig with it!

The pilot retrieved the gun from the canopy and brought it to her. She began swinging it butt first into the snow.

He was relieved to see she'd removed the magazine.

"That's no way to treat a weapon," he told her as she battered and scraped the surface of the rubble with the assault rifle.

Mun knew better.

Even though this was a Chinese Type 47, it was still a Kalishnikov. A long time ago a *kwai lo* from Russia had designed this weapon to take just this abuse.

Mun struck something. She scraped at it with the barrel. There was a metallic sound, and the pilot moved in for a better look.

Mun flipped the thing with the AK's barrel.

At first it looked like a rock. But it wasn't a rock. It was a chunk of concrete with a piece of drop-forged steel sticking out of it.

Mun smiled. She had found a piece of the vault's entrance.

The rubble splayed from the ravine wall in a V, so it was easy to tell where the threshold would be under all that snow. There were several large rock slabs slightly above her on the slope in the location of the vault's door.

Mun was impatient to enter it.

"We'll need your cable," she told the pilot. "We have to move that." The pilot rolled his eyes. Mun Giyang was pointing at the largest of the rock slabs.

"We'll come back," he said reasonably. "We've only got fifteen minutes' worth of fuel, and there's nothing to shore up the rock once we move it."

"It only takes five minutes to get back to the airport," Mun snapped. "You move the rock and I'll shore it up."

"How?" His disbelief had turned into humor. The man was now smirking at her.

"Do it." Mun said threateningly.

The rock moved easily. The pilot had fitted the cable around its narrowest point. He pulled the slab skyward till there was a gaping hole in the ground. Mun looked in.

Despite the long shadows, she could see a long gallery stacked with wooden crates. She had done it!

She only allowed herself a quick look. The thought of the rock slab hanging over her head speeded her movements. Mun struggled with a small rock, pushing and rolling it through the broken snow till it rested beside a second and much larger rock.

The second rock was about halfway up the slope. It had been slightly to the side of the slab that the helicopter was still holding.

With her assault rifle braced against the first rock, Mun levered this second one till it lapped over the gaping hole. She cleared out quickly and motioned for the pilot to descend.

The slab was lowered. Mun's idea worked. She released the cable and preened herself in front of the hovering helicopter.

The pilot began to think how unpleasant her company was going to be on the ride home....

STRASSKO CAME PUFFING up the ramp of the transport cursing Soviet technology. He thought of the expensive Western cars he had passed his idle moments drooling over many weeks ago in Montreal.

That buffoon Goroslov would go into his report. The man had issued Strassko a Skaldia whose pistons had not fired in sync since 1923!

The foul machine had broken down three times on the way to the plane. He would have done much better, Strassko reflected, to have obeyed his first instincts and ridden in the truck with the peasant Zom and his helper.

He hoped nothing had happened to his precious cargo. Strassko finally stood in the belly of the plane and rested from the climb up the ramp.

When his breathing returned to normal, he saw Dr. Kanamuto's crate.

Again he knocked on it.

Again there was a response.

Strassko stood back to consider the crate for the first time. It really was a breakthrough in intelligence technology. Basically it was a large space suit. It did not carry its own oxygen but it did carry a ventilator, a humidifier and was equipped to handle the liquid wastes that the occupant would pass during his confinement.

Since the occupant was only fed liquids, this worked out well.

Strassko knew that the crate had been designed by the same team who had designed the cosmonauts' most recent suits. He had used such crates before, but he had never been on hand when one was opened. Molinz had advised him to stand downwind if he ever found himself in such a position.

Strassko wondered how the Soviet Union could produce something of such sophistication and still produce a car like that Skaldia. He punched the heel of his hand into the ramp's up button and listened to the hydraulics' whine. Metal rattled in the wind as the ramp climbed toward the transport's belly, but Strassko could not hear it.

He was already ahead, shouting to the crew. Bolan heard the ramp slam home and the words ''late'' and ''takeoff'' come out of the cockpit far ahead of him.

Both engines on the right wing started up. Seconds later the left ones started. From inside the crate Bolan could feel the motion as the transport turned on the airstrip.

Now they were taxiing. Bolan was forced back against the engine as the transport lifted off the ground. Again he felt the plane turn, and he knew that finally they were headed south into China.

WITH THE ROCK SLAB WEDGED, Mun was through the hole into Kanamuto's vault before her pilot could land. She could not control her impatience. But she should have.

Before she had gone half a dozen steps, her improvised portal slammed shut behind her. A boulder the size of a melon hurtled down the irregular incline. Mun could hear it, but there was nowhere to turn. It caught her in her left kidney with an explosion of pain so intense that her ears hurt from the noise of the stone as it rattled past her.

Then the gray shadows turned black....

From the air Mun's pilot could see her duck into the chasm they had exposed. Idiot, he thought. She cannot wait!

He said a lot of other things. He was just running out of things to say when the weight of the stone slab disappeared. The helicopter shot up vertically. He gained twenty meters before he grabbed the stick and held her. Beside him he could see the cable curling like a snapped elastic.

It was okay, Mun's pilot told himself. The cable had simply pulled loose of the slab.

He could reconnect it without the woman's help. He had enough fuel to lift it again. He would lift from the air while Mun crawled to safety. It would be interesting to see if the little accident improved her personality.

He hoped it would. They would have to spend some time together waiting to be picked up. The fuel was very low.

Mun's pilot scanned the horizon in the direction of the Harbin airport. From the quality of the late-afternoon light, he had been able to tell for a few hours that a storm was coming. But that had been the last thing on his mind.

Now as he looked toward Harbin in the west, the pilot could see the dense gray cloud of a real blizzard closing in on them. It would not touch them until dark, but he was glad he had looked. It was just another factor in what had turned into a perfect day, he thought wryly.

He tried for the first time to raise Harbin Airport. He got a lot of air traffic but no response. First things first, he told himself, and fastened the cable once more around the slab of rock....

THE STINK INSIDE THE BOX WAS AWFUL. At first there had been the faint odor of urine. Vesh could handle that. He was a sailor. Strong smells were part of the sea.

Much more disturbing than the dead man's piss was the dead man himself. Vesh knew he was sitting in the Oriental's lap trussed up like a spool of twine.

He didn't know what was going on with Mack Bolan. He had no idea what the game was that he had been unlucky enough to walk into. But now, in the lap of a dead man, Vesh could not help thinking that he would be the next to die.

I will need all my wits, he decided. I'll have to spot my chance when it comes and make the best of it.

Incredibly, he was not entirely helpless. The American who had eyes in the back of his head had not felt that Vesh Slovincik was much of a threat. He had left the palm gun in the man's boot. If I get my hands free before they kill me, Vesh decided, I have a small chance.

The thought was a comfort to him inside the box for the first two days. Then Dr. Kanamuto began to smell. The smell just got worse from then on. Vesh always felt like puking. He had found the suckling container of liquid food on the crate wall at just about mouth height. But after those first few days he could eat nothing.

It's like being buried alive, Vesh thought. But it was worse.

He could feel the roll and pitch of the ship, and he knew that less than six inches of wall separated him from the outside world. It was maddening to think he was that close to escape!

It's like being entombed, Vesh thought. Except that it was worse than that because his wrists and legs ached from the ropes that bound him.

It's like...Vesh groped for more points of comparison. And with each one he decided his situation was worse, much worse.

This was the way he amused himself until he arrived in China.

There had been high points on the trip. He had felt the motion of being off-loaded by the dockworkers in Vladivostok. His heart pounded when the crate containing him shot out of the hold like a bullet from a gun. And when the webbing tore on the side of the hold, Vesh felt the crate sliding and knew at last that death had come for him.

There was also an occasional knocking on the side of the crate. The Yugoslav sailor was convinced the person knocking was a sadist. The man never gave any response. But each time he knocked, Vesh answered as he was sure Dr. Kanamuto would have answered by knocking his forehead against the crate's padded side.

Now there was motion again. In the dark Vesh strained his ears, but nothing penetrated the thick wall of the crate. What this place needs, Vesh suddenly thought in a flash of good spirits, is a phone.

That's it, he decided. This place is like a phone booth. He laughed at his discovery and made the mistake of inhaling deeply. No, he decided. It's not like a phone booth. It's worse.

"CAN YOU HEAR ME?" he was shouting at a rock, hoping his voice would be able to reach the woman in the cavern behind it.

"Can you hear?" There was no answer. He grabbed the AK's magazine and tapped on the flat part of the stone.

Still nothing....

A wave of fear hit the pilot for the first time. If that stupid woman had hurt herself, the pilot thought, he would fly night duty in Tibet for the next thirty years.

She couldn't be dead! He squeezed the thought out of his mind and slammed the magazine down hard on the stone.

Nothing.

Okay, I'm going to do it, anyway, he decided. He moved back to the helicopter, slipping his rifle's magazine into his pocket as he went.

There was not much fuel left. Maybe more than five minutes' worth, but he knew that takeoff, landing and lifting all required more fuel than simply flying.

I can get it up, he decided. And I can lift that damn rock. What I can't do is make that stupid, willful woman leave the cave or the money.

Let's do it, he thought, and the bird lifted off....

LING HAD NEVER MET the Soviet general before, but there was no mistaking the man who stepped off the Moscow-Peking train seconds after it stopped in the Harbin station.

He was tall and gaunt with an impassive gray face that hardened into a cruel mouth. He wore no uniform but the ankle-length gray tweed coat replaced insignia. It emphasized the man's height and presence.

"Is that him?" Ling's driver asked.

"Yes."

The man left the waiting sedan and hurried toward the general.

The Soviet master spy turned his attention toward the small uniformed figure with a curt nod of acknowledgment. The driver offered to carry his bags but Strakhov retained them. He brushed past the youth and walked to Ling's car.

The driver ran after him and opened the door.

Wordlessly Strakhov entered. "You are Ling," he said to the old man inside. Ling nodded.

They remained silent for a long time. Uncomfortably silent, thought the driver, as he started the machine.

"What kind of car is this?" Strakhov began.

"You couldn't pronounce it," Ling told him.

"Dr. Kanamuto will arrive tomorrow," Strakhov said after a while.

Ling nodded. "Han will drop you at your quarters."

Han kept his eyes away from the rearview mirror. He wondered if either man in the back seat was armed.

7

Mack Bolan lifted the lid of the crated engine and stole a look down the length of the motionless plane.

He could hear voices in an Oriental language coming from the direction of the ramp and the occasional curse word that he knew meant Strassko was off-loading Dr. Kanamuto.

He let the lid down gently and returned to the velvety darkness that had held him for four hours. When the noises stilled, Bolan again raised the lid of the crate and looked in the direction of the ramp.

It was closed now. There was an empty space beside it where Dr. Kanamuto's crate had stood. But the smaller box was still there. Bolan began to raise the lid but froze when he detected a plume of steam, exhaled air from someone standing guard over the small crate.

He could not see the guard, but the distance that separated them was a good four and a half meters. It was going to be hard getting out of the box and closing the gap between them before that sentry noticed, Bolan thought. He needed an edge.

The Executioner took the Magnum from his shoulder rig and pushed against the lid of the crate. He let in just enough light to allow him to see that the chamber was clear.

Then he tapped against the wood with the barrel. Lightly at first. When there was no reaction, he tapped again.

One. Two.

His eyes faced the plume of exhaled breath. From under the small gap in the lid he could see the vapor of breath pause and turn in his direction.

He waited.

The breath vapor turned back.

Bolan tapped the barrel against the surface of the wood again. He paced the taps evenly but added a third one. One. Two. Three.

Again the plume of breath stopped and turned toward him.

Again he waited till it turned back.

Then he tapped some more, tapping faintly. One. Two.

He knew exactly what was going on inside the guard's head. He was giving the bored man something to focus on. Sooner or later, he'll check it out. Bolan knew that from experience.

He didn't have to wait too long. With the next set of taps, the man came away from his resting place and Mack Bolan got his first glimpse of him.

The man wore the uniform of an Aeroflot crew member. He looked to be about Bolan's size, and for this the Executioner was grateful. He wanted the man's clothing because he needed a cover. A Westerner in an obscure part of China would stand out like a naked man in a bank.

The guard came close to Bolan's side of the crate but not close enough. His head was turned away, but he was still too far to be jumped with any guarantee of success.

Mack Bolan tapped again.

This time the guard realized the faint noise was coming from inside the amidships crate. He lifted the lid and stuck his head inside. When it came back out it had a pistol jammed into its nose.

It felt good to stand up at last. Mack Bolan kept his gun trained on the Soviet airman as he exited the box, swinging one leg over the side at a time. The man stood against the bulkhead with his hands raised.

Bolan noticed he was not breathing as much.

"Okay, strip!" the Executioner told the man. "Strip!" he repeated in Russian, gesturing with the AutoMag.

The Russian stripped.

HE HAD BEEN on a truck again. Vesh was certain of that. Then he had been lifted up some stairs, many stairs. They had carried him backward, and the blood had come rushing to his head.

Now he was being wheeled backward. There was a sharp corner that was taken very fast. He came to a stop suddenly. There was no thump as the crate struck the floor but he felt a sudden jerk and Vesh imagined there was a thump.

It's like being caught in the surf in a very small boat, Vesh decided.

A crowbar entered the side seam of the crate beside his head, letting in a little light. A second crowbar entered the opposite side.

With the light came some fresh air. Vesh strained toward it and sucked it in.

Then the front of the crate came off.

Vesh recognized one man as the passenger from the *Tito I*. His eyes were caught and held, however, by the second man, a man with a face like a hawk, a brutal man. Vesh backed away from that face with an exaggerated caution.

The surprised face followed him. "Strassko!" it said in sharp, merciless Russian. "What is this?" Suddenly the face made a grimace and pulled back from the crate.

It does not smell *that* bad, Vesh thought. He looked at the one called Strassko who was standing in the far corner of the room with a handkerchief over his mouth.

There were tears in his eyes.

Vesh turned back toward the first one who had produced a large clasp knife and was approaching the crate. He did not like the look in that one's pale eyes.

This is definitely bad, Vesh told himself.

"Kanamuto is dead!" the dangerous one said when he got closer. "Who is this?" he was shouting over his shoulder.

"A sailor from the freighter," the second man said meekly. "Nobody."

Vesh saw the man's knife hand snake toward him. He felt the sharp point under his chin where it broke the skin, and even though he pulled away from it, it followed him till his head was backed into the far corner of the crate.

"Where is Dolan?" the voice said.

More than anything Vesh wished he knew what Bolan was.

MUN CAME TO AFTER A DISTURBING nightmare that she was an unborn child in the belly of a woman who had just died.

Kanamuto's vault was cold and absolutely black. She was lying on her back with her feet uphill from her head. She didn't know how long she'd been unconscious, but it felt like only a few minutes.

Absentmindedly she tried to roll onto her right side, but a wave of pain caught her and washed her back onto the ground.

Now she remembered.

Stupidly she had rushed into the cave before the pilot had landed. If she had waited a few moments longer, her wedge would have collapsed with her still on the *outside* of the cave. If it hadn't been for her own willfulness she would still be free to act.

"I'm an idiot!" Mun shouted into the dark.

It hurt to shout.

She passed what seemed like a long time before she heard a metallic tapping on the stone ahead of her. She groped in the dark till she found a small stone. With it she tried to reply to her pilot's taps.

Get me out of here. Please, get me out! Mun tried to think of the man's name, but she remembered embarrassedly that she had never used it. Worse, when she tried to think of his face she could not bring it to mind.

"What is your name?" she imagined asking him, and she imagined he answered, "Captain X."

She laughed at the absurd name for a moment. Then she became serious. I'm feverish, Mun thought. I'm badly hurt.

A wave of self-pity passed over her. Ordinarily she would have given in to it, but she now knew it was exactly that kind of self-indulgence that had gotten her into this jam in the first place. "Be strong!" she shouted at no one.

Above her the rock slab lifted.

She felt the cold air before she saw the light. The cold air blew in under the rock, carrying gusts of the powdery snow that stung and melted on her forehead and hands. The light hit a spot in the vault directly above her head. As the rock slab lifted, the light continued to grow backward toward the entrance. She could now see her own feet.

Above her she could hear the thwupping sound of Captain X's helicopter. She knew he had little fuel left. She knew she had to move fast.

Mun Giyang tried to turn uphill. The pain from her left kidney became intense. She ignored it and spun around on her rear. Now she was facing back down the cave. She rolled onto her front and began to crawl toward the light.

The crawling didn't come easily. Although her legs were working, sne found it hard to move her left side because any effort twisted the back muscles that already ached.

She tried crawling, using her arms and right leg. That seemed to gain her some ground and she kept it up. The slope, which had seemed a minor thing when the light first entered, now seemed as high as any of the hills around Harbin.

She knew she was short on the numbers. Captain X had kept the rock slab lifted for a long time, and he must be running short of fuel. Mun Giyang pushed forward for all she was worth. She barely had any strength left, and there was still so far to go.

"Please wait!" she shouted. "Wait for me!"

There were three meters left to crawl and they were slippery. The rotors were creating a down draft that blew loose snow under the lip of the rock above her.

He still can't see me, Mun thought. She lost about a meter as she slid back down through the snow. She was sobbing now. Out of control but still fighting against the pain, against the slope, against the numbers.

She got higher than she had been before she slipped when she slipped for the second time.

This time Mun stayed motionless on the rock face. "Please help me!" she wailed.

Overhead the pilot lowered the stone.

"YOU'RE PARANOID!" Strassko shouted at Strakhov. He was surprised at his own boldness.

Strakhov turned back toward his subordinate with the look a predator gives to the thing it is going to eat. "Shut up, Strassko," he said very quietly.

Strassko felt his blood turn cold.

Strakhov turned back toward Vesh Slovincik. The knife was still pressed tight into the man's jaw. An irregular line of blood had dripped onto the blade and now touched Strakhov's index finger. Vesh's face was contorted, as though he were trying to pull all his flesh to the other side of his face, the side away from Strakhov's little knife.

"The man who tied you up," Strakhov said in the same lethally quiet voice, "what did he look like?"

Vesh described the Executioner.

"Good," Strakhov said. "Now, why did he kill Dr. Kanamuto?"

Vesh did not understand, and Strakhov's impatience showed. "The dead man you're sitting on is Dr. Kanamuto. Did Bolan kill him?"

Vesh understood. Bolan was a who, not a what. He shook his head at Strakhov. "His neck was broken when we found him."

Strakhov was still unsure. "So he was already dead?"

Vesh's mind whirled. Strakhov had wanted something from Kanamuto, that was clear. If Vesh could figure out what it was he might be able to stay alive long enough to get his hands on his gun. Vesh took a chance. "I didn't say he was dead," he told Strakhov. "I said his neck was broken. The man you call Bolan thought he was dead when he stuffed me in here."

"Was he alive?" Strakhov demanded. His anger with the sailor's pussyfooting was showing now in his eyes. Vesh had seen these eyes before, but only in prison.

"Briefly," he said, sneering at Strakhov. "Now take that damn thing out of my neck or I'll never take you there." Vesh smiled. It was a huge risk, but it was the only way available. He knew he had to carry it off with class. Suddenly the sailor was discovering his strength. It felt good to talk to the general like that.

Strakhov appraised the man again. "You can lead us to the germs?"

Vesh suspected the man might be trying to trick him. "He didn't say what. He just said where." The Yugoslav paused. "Free me and I'll take you there."

"Which entrance is it?" Strakhov asked him suspiciously. Searchers for the germs had concentrated on two entrances to the ice caves that were both roughly five kilometers from the testing facility.

Vesh said nothing.

"He's lying," Strassko said across the room. "He just wants to stay alive. He knows nothing."

"Shut up!" Strakhov yelled over his shoulder. "Is it Kai-bin or Wah-ling?" He demanded. Vesh burned both names into his memory.

"He knows shit!" Strassko said behind them. But Strakhov wanted to believe.

"If you *really* know," he told Vesh, "you know that we need you to lead us through the caves. The name is nothing. I just want to hear you say it."

"Kai-bin," Vesh said in a flat voice.

"Impossible!" Strakhov said.

"Bullshit," Strassko said in English.

Vesh just smiled. Strakhov spent minutes studying his smile. Finally he took the knife away from the sailor's throat and cut the ropes on his legs and chest. The hands he left bound together.

"General," Strassko said behind him, "this man is lying." In fact Strassko *knew* that Vesh was lying. During his interrogation in Brooklyn, Dr. Kanamuto had revealed that the way to the vault lay through neither the Kai-bin nor Wah-ling caves.

Dr. Kanamuto had told him that the Japanese had destroyed the entrance to their cave with the same dynamite they had used to ruin the testing facility.

Strassko believed Kanamuto. The man had been desperate to spare his niece.

Strange, the KGB man thought, for that much tenderness to be contained in a war criminal.

"This man is lying," Strassko repeated.

Strakhov turned to face him.

"Comrade Strassko," the general said, smiling, "you have disappointed me. Dr. Kanamuto was in your care and now we are put in the position of needing a man you correctly identify as untrustworthy. We have very little time available to us," he reminded Strassko. "The Chinese won't tolerate our presence for very much longer."

"All the more reason we shouldn't get sidetracked by phonies," Strassko insisted. "General," he said in exasperation, "I *know* what this man says is untrue."

"Do you also know where the germs are?" Strakhov asked flatly.

It wasn't really a question. The general didn't wait for an answer.

"I think I made the decision to give you Molinz's job too quickly—you are relieved."

Strassko's face was a stone that gave nothing away. He nodded in submission, but the cruel line of his mouth as he looked at Greb Strakhov suggested the fight had just started.

Vesh winked at him as he left the room....

8

Mack Bolan let the Russian crew member don the Executioner's own pea jacket before tying him up inside the transport's crated engine. He didn't need to kill the man, and it was not in him to let the Soviet freeze.

Bolan himself took the Russian's down-filled parka and moved along the transport toward the smaller second crate.

Once more he opened it. This time, however, he strained over the lid of the crate, spreading the paper packing until the entire device was exposed.

Then Bolan lifted the thing out of its packing. As he'd anticipated, it had straps on the far, flat side, like the straps on a backpack. Bolan gripped it carefully and slung it onto his back. He punched the hydraulic ramp's button with the butt end of the Magnum and listened for the noises of being discovered over the whine and rattle of the ramp.

There was no alarm. The ramp banged home, and Bolan walked down it confidently, taking in the airfield scene as he walked. When his eyes cleared the interior of the transport he could see an empty truck not twenty meters from the left wing.

There were no people anywhere near him.

Bolan made the right turn naturally and walked across the tarmac of the curtain, studying the setting.

The Chinese sky was somber. Bolan knew that despite the subzero bite in the air it would soon snow. For that reason there was no traffic arriving or departing Harbin. The controllers' tower, a small glass booth atop a concrete pillar, was empty.

The only visible personnel outside the terminus buildings were those guarding the service and freight gates, the gates through which Bolan knew he would have to pass.

He shucked his burden when he reached the truck and slipped it onto the passenger seat. He could feel the eyes of the guards at the gate on him as he walked casually around the front of the truck and entered the cab.

He knew they were cold and bored. He hoped their interest was just a casual one. Even so, the Executioner withdrew Big Thunder and slid it under his right leg so he could retrieve it easily.

He had a bit of luck. The truck was a button starter. He didn't need a key. He pushed it and the engine turned over reluctantly, making the choked, nasal sound of pistons trying to fire in a cold block.

The wha-wha-wha of the motor raised the guards' heads. They had ignored Bolan when he had entered the cab but now he was once again the focus of their attention.

"Damn!" Still the truck wouldn't start.

One of the PLA guards slung his carbine and began walking toward Bolan. The Executioner felt the pressure of the Magnum under his leg, but he resolved not to use it unless things got desperate.

A second guard had also slung his rifle and was walking out across the airstrip after the first. He called through the cold air toward the first man good-naturedly. Bolan could see the crooked line of his teeth as the engine caught and revved.

The second man, still very close to the gate, stopped walking and exclaimed to no one. Bolan couldn't decipher the sounds but he knew the meaning had to be, "It's okay now."

The first guard was past the halfway point. He continued walking toward the Executioner's truck. Bolan revved the engine violently, trying to get it as warm as he could in the few moments left. He just didn't need the damn thing to stall on him....

Clouds of white engine exhaust surrounded the cab in the brittle air. Through the dense, swirling smoke, Bolan kept his eyes constantly on the PLA guard. The man was still approaching.

He had to take the initiative.

Bolan let the high-revving motor calm down. He put the truck in gear but the clutch, too, was near freezing. The gears ground, making the closest guard wince. The stick popped forward in his hand.

The Executioner's face remained impassive. He pushed in the clutch and shifted into gear. Smoothly.

All right, he decided. Let's do it.

Mack Bolan coasted slowly across the tarmac. The PLA soldier was slightly to the left of his cab and Bolan coolly turned toward him so that the man's face came up to the driver's window.

The man smiled and said something unintelligible. He made the wha-wha-wha sound, then the crunching noise of the gearshift.

"Yeah," Bolan said in Russian. "It sure is cold."

The Chinese grinned. He made a big cloud of smoke with his breath and pointed at it.

"Cold. Sure thing," Bolan said.

Satisfied with their exchange, the PLA guard mounted the cab's running board and held on to the mirror beside

Bolan. He motioned for the Executioner to drive to the gate, which a third man was now opening.

Mack Bolan tried hard not to smile. "Sure thing," he told the uncomprehending soldier. "I'll just drive through that gate and catch you later. Don't wait up for me."

As Bolan edged forward, the second PLA guard approached from the right. He too climbed onto the cab's running boards. On the passenger's side, however, he was immediately confronted with the strange backpack lying across the seat.

He gestured toward it and made an inquiring series of sounds.

"Oh, you know," Bolan told him in a casual tone of voice, "just a couple of things I picked up for the missus."

The second guard stood on tiptoe and shouted over the roof to his companion. The man strained to catch the words as they blew over the truck toward him. Then he crouched beside the window and peered into the cab.

The gate was almost entirely open now but the Executioner knew his guard wasn't saying, "Hey, chum, what you got there?" He smiled and shrugged, taking his hands off the wheel briefly. As he suspected it would, the truck pulled badly to the left.

He gunned it. The first guard fell off onto the tarmac. The noise of his assault rifle clattering was lost in the high whine of the engine surging in a low gear. The truck bucked as Mack Bolan took back the wheel and shifted into a higher gear, but the sudden lurch was not enough to lose the second man.

Bolan would have to try again.

He turned toward the passenger window, catching sight of the guard pulling on the assault rifle on his back. It was awkward but the man was having some success.

Bolan turned his eyes frontward again and grabbed under his leg for the Magnum. The third man on the gate was now closing it. Bolan needed to focus his eyes to the front, but he was certainly aware of the threat of the man to his right.

The Executioner's eyes didn't leave the road as he snapped off a round at the second man. At the sound of the shots the man on the gate stopped pulling and started shooting.

The truck's windshield spiderwebbed from a 3-round burst. When Bolan's head cleared the steering wheel, he saw the third man run for cover. He was almost on top of Bolan.

The wounded guard still clung on to the passenger side of the truck. Bolan had had enough of him.

He swung sharply to the right as the truck met the gate and the chain link came free from the post, with the contact whipping the second PLA guard away to the side.

Bolan batted the impacted glass from the windshield with the barrel of the AutoMag. He felt a surge of relief when he could finally see clearly but it was short-lived. The cold winter air streaming through the cab tore at his eyes till they teared and froze on his cheeks.

He squinted his face into the wind, placed the Magnum once more beneath his right leg and forced the stick into a higher gear.

Mack Bolan wondered if there was such a thing as a car chase in China. He knew he was damn sure going to find out....

CAPTAIN X'S REAL NAME WAS HU, and Hu was in big trouble.

He had lifted the slab of rock for as long as he could without crashing. The girl had not come out.

Hu knew something had happened to her inside the cave. He had no way of getting to her, and now the radio offered not even the reassuring salad of voices he had picked up earlier.

The storm front was moving in. It was almost on top of him. He radioed a Mayday over and over again but got no response. There would be no help for them tonight. He knew he could not walk across the Harbin hills to the airport. The blizzard would be on him in less than an hour.

Hu busied himself getting ready for the storm. Each PLA helicopter had a medical chest stashed under the pilot's seat. Hu withdrew it now as he stood in the snow beside the bird.

He set the black metal case on the floor beside the stick and itemized its contents. There was a lot of surgical gauze, iodine, sutures and such that he knew would come in handy if he was ever able to reach Mun.

There was also an American K-Bar knife, two space blankets and a bottle of rubbing alcohol.

Hu took the K-bar and walked down the outside of the chopper, letting the isinglass pilot's door flap closed behind him. The wind was bitter while he busied himself at the power pack. Hu hoped that the temperature would go up slightly when it began to snow.

That was the way it usually worked, he told himself. He tore a two-meter length of hose off the fuel pump with the K-bar and returned to the enclosed canopy.

Again with his knife, Hu separated the lid of the medical chest from the box itself. He rummaged around in the snow till he found an assortment of fist-sized rocks.

He patiently brushed the snow from the rocks and chipped the little pockets of ice from their uneven surfaces. He intended to use them to retain heat and he knew that a wet, steam heat from these rocks would quickly soak him through. If I get wet, Hu thought cheerfully, I die.

Hu took both seats out of the canopy and set the metal medical box in front of the stick. He filled the box with stones, then tore the wrapper from the first of the space blankets and stretched it around the plastic canopy until Hu could only see his own reflection through the front of the craft. There was enough of the silver material to entirely cover the doors, too, but Hu left them partly uncovered. He still needed to come and go at will, and they were the only way left to see outside.

Hu stood inside the canopy, making a tear in the space blanket directly above the metal box. He took a pack of Pear Tree chewing gum from his flyer's jacket and stuffed three pieces into his mouth. The sharp aroma of pear and ginger filled his nose. As he worked inside the small space of the canopy, Hu stopped periodically and stuffed more gum into his mouth.

Soon the ginger was making his eyes water. Hu laughed as he knelt over the box. He brushed the tears away with a gloved hand and watched them fall and freeze on a corner of the silver sheeting.

Next Hu hammered down the corners of the medical box's lid. When it was a flat surface, he gripped the sheet of metal in both hands and twisted, making a funnel of it.

Hu stood again and took the huge wad of yellow gum from his mouth. He stuck it into the spot above his head where he had cut through the blanket. Then he attached the length of hose to the chewing gum.

Hu applied pressure on the hose and the gum until they were securely frozen to the canopy.

The hose now dangled directly over the metal box.

When he was certain that the hose was frozen inside the gum, Hu attached the metal funnel to the dangling end. He put the other end outside the highest corner of the canopy door.

Now he had a chimney.

All he needed was something to burn.

Hu took the K-bar outside and tore the stuffing out of the helicopter chairs. It was not enough, not nearly enough to last him the long, cold night ahead.

Hu looked around the ravine where the useless helicopter rested. He knew that in the summer this area was choked with scrub. Now most of it lay dead beneath the snow. But here and there the gray branches of the withered hom bushes stuck out of the brittle white blanket.

It would be a trade-off, Hu realized. He was thinking of his feet. He had come poorly dressed for walking through deep snow. The People's Liberation Army issued its personnel no boots.

Soldiers wore a kind of high-cut sneaker that was comparable to the Israeli combat boot, though less well made. As he started to gather the visible twigs of hom, Hu could feel his feet getting colder and colder.

They will be wet long before I make the fire, he decided.

He wanted to put off burning anything until dark. It was subzero weather, but Hu knew he would be warm enough until the light gave out. Night would be the big challenge.

His arms filled with wood, Hu returned to the chopper and loaded his prize inside the canopy.

Then he tore the wrapper on the second space blanket.

With the sutures from the medical chest, Hu made a makeshift sleeping bag, open at both ends. He placed one of the gutted chair frames directly in front of the fire and wrapped the space blanket completely around its edges.

Now when he crawled inside his bag he'd have central heating at his feet.

It might work, Hu told himself. It just might work.

From the medical supplies Hu selected the bottle of rubbing alcohol. He tipped some over the bare stones in his "fireplace" and tested the design. The reflectors caught the small heat of the alcohol and sent it back to him greatly increased.

Hu did not feel warm, but at last he believed that he was going to survive the night. He tipped the bottle of alcohol to his mouth and took a swig. It tasted better than all that ginger.

But it was a close thing.

STRASSKO SPENT THE EVENING going over maps and a copy of a report by some government geologist called Shu.

If I am to save my position, he told himself, *I* must be the one to find the germs.

He did have a slight edge. Bright and early tomorrow Strakhov would be off with that fool sailor to the Kai-bin caves.

In the report in front of him Strassko read everything about the Kai-bin caves. It had cost the Soviets a small fortune to steal the report. Strassko's translation was one of only two copies. It had previously belonged to Colonel Molinz.

Kai-bin, he already knew, was the less favored of the two closest *known* entrances to the Harbin ice caves. These entrances were a meager five kilometers from the testing facility.

The next nearest entrance was an additional six kilometers away.

Both the Kai-bin and Wah-ling entrances led downward in a rough V but Kai-bin's angle was less steep, so it was commonly held to be less deep.

That's why Strakhov was surprised at the sailor's choice, Strassko thought.

The report before him, however, stated that both entrances converged at the Great Shu ravine, a long underground trench like the ones visible in the Harbin hills.

By constantly bearing right from the Kai-bin entrance and left from the Wah-ling entrance, two cave explorers would be able to see each other's lights after an hour of easy descent. If both explorers continued to follow the ravine they would eventually meet in a gallery with five descending exits.

Only two of the exits had ever been explored. Both led to the right, the direction, Shu's report pointed out, of the testing facility. Neither one had produced any interesting results.

Knowing now that Strakhov had not read the report, Strassko suddenly hoped that he and the sailor would blunder into one of the explored galleries on a path that would waste their time and increase Strassko's advantage.

He turned from the report to a contour map of the terrain surrounding Harbin. In this map, the city lay south and west in the bottom left corner. To the right was the airport and, nearby, the Kai-bin entrance.

The Wah-ling entrance was farther east. Together, both caves formed the base of an equilateral triangle. The Japanese Imperial Testing Facility nestled five kilometers north of the hills holding these caves.

Now Strassko studied the contour lines where the space between them increased near the testing facility. It was just possible that the same geological disturbance that made the caves would leave a trace on the surface.

Provided you knew where to look.

Strassko poured some green Chinese tea from the stainless-steel pot in front of him. It was terrible, watery stuff.

Involuntarily he glanced at the top of the map toward Irkutsk. His few hours in Vladivostok had been his first steps on Soviet soil in more than a year. Sergei Strassko did not like many things about Mother Russia, but they did make good tea.

His eyes still glued to the map, Strassko reached into the left drawer of the desk and withdrew Strakhov's own bottle of vodka. He unscrewed the aluminum cap and poured freely into the cup containing the watery tea.

Some vodka spilled on the map, and Strassko finally took his attention away from the location of the testing facility.

His vodka, Strassko thought mockingly. If all goes well, I will take his job, too.

The KGB agent dipped the third finger of his right hand toward the map. It came away wet with vodka. Strassko stuck it between his teeth on the right side of his jaw and once again studied the map while he sucked the strong liquor.

The scent of the vodka made him think of Kanamuto's rotting corpse. The air in the room had been sharp with the smell of the dead man.

He had clearly underestimated Bolan. The Executioner had been useful to him in disposing of Molinz, but now the man was becoming dangerous.

Strassko suddenly imagined that the Executioner would arrive and kill General Strakhov. That would solve all my problems, he thought.

He laughed at himself, removing his finger from his mouth and filling the cold air in front of him with his thin wispy breath.

I am a child, he thought, knowing that only a child would dream of someone solving a problem for him. I am too old for parents, Strassko thought good-humoredly. Besides, although the man had the cunning to get onto the freighter, he could never follow us to China.

Strassko was sure of it.

He turned his attention back toward the map.

The road from the airport, he noticed, led directly past the Wah-ling cave.

9

The People's Liberation Army didn't waste any time.

The Executioner had floored the accelerator, heading in the direction of the road signs. He turned a curve past the airport and saw the lights of a city on the horizon under the blackening cowl of storm cloud.

He also saw the roadblock.

Farther ahead in a spot where the soft shoulders disappeared abruptly into slit trenches, two khaki trucks like the one he was driving were parked across the road in an overlapping V.

Good place for a roadblock, Bolan thought.

There was no way around it and there was no way through it. Mack Bolan picked his spot in a place where the soft shoulder spread out expansively. He pulled a 180-degree turn easily.

When the truck leveled out he eased up a bit, careful not to fishtail the thing.

Bolan wanted no accidents to prevent him from delivering his parcel.

Wind from the window tore at the left side of his face. He turned his head out of it, squinting through his right eye into the gathering dusk.

As he did so he could see the airport passing on his left. The second wounded soldier was still on the ground but the one farther away, the one Bolan had had the conversation with, was standing.

He saw the Executioner's truck spurting past the destroyed gate and dived for his gun. Bolan could hear the kick and whine of a burst of automatic fire, but none of the slugs came near him.

He couldn't see the man anymore in the driver's side mirror. What he did see was two trucks.

The Executioner turned his attention back to the road. Here he was in China, he thought, in a car chase, headed in the wrong direction with a blizzard coming in at him any minute.

There was a good chance, he decided, that things could not get worse.

It was a comforting thought, a slight moment of relief in the brutal course he had chosen. Mack Bolan looked ahead toward the hills whose dark shapes loomed above the level plain.

Maybe I can lose them ahead, he thought.

He shifted into a lower gear and began climbing at about the time they got close enough to shoot....

HIS FOOT WAS JUST LIKE THE OTHER ONE, puffy and tender. He should never have tramped around in the snow. It had been necessary, sure. He needed the wood to stay alive.

He just wished he'd had better shoes.

The puffiness, Hu knew, was the first telltale sign of frostbite. When the skin froze, some of the cells broke open and left the feet swollen.

If the feet remained cold and untreated they would go gangrenous in a day.

Hu imagined sitting in the helicopter trying to amputate his toes with the K-bar. Things were nowhere near that bad, he knew, but his imagination played with him to fill the empty hours in front of his dismal little fire.

He rubbed the cold skin gingerly to restore the circulation. He brought his foot as close to the fire as he could without burning it and sat with his foot in midair.

His hands were now occupied cupping some of the rubbing alcohol. It was cold from the bottle. Hu knew it would have to be lukewarm before he could apply it to his foot to restore the circulation.

He rubbed it in with a will, focusing on this small task to take his bored mind off the grim images that he was only too able to invent.

Ah, that's better, he thought, feeling the sting of the alcohol on his tender skin. The heat from the fire was good, too. A few drops spilled and burned, but Hu was very careful not to bring his skin anywhere near the flame.

"Stupid I'm not," Hu told himself aloud. He looked up from his foot almost as soon as he'd spoken. He could have sworn he'd heard another noise at the same instant.

Hu took his foot away from the flame. He strained his ears but all he could place were storm noises, wind howling and whipping around the canopy and the tail, the vibration of the heavy rotors bobbing in the wind, the wet snow impacting on everything and being compacted by its own weight.

Nothing.

Hu spoke again, trying to assess his memory of the sound he'd made against the same set of sounds. "Stupid I'm not," he said.

It wasn't the same.

He didn't know why it was so important to him to identify the sounds. I'm just bored, he decided. He turned his attention back to his foot.

Then he heard it again.

The hungry sound traveled toward him on the force of the wind. He stiffened. The skin on his neck tingled. He rolled over in the space-blanket sleeping bag and pressed the canopy door an inch or two wider than the gap left in it by his chimney.

Wolves.

Two or three of them, at least, Hu decided. There was no telling how far away they were. A wind like this could drown a sound immediately or it could pick it up and make it travel.

Between these two extremes, Hu knew, was an infinite number of possibilities. I'll just have to hope they're not close enough to smell my wood smoke, he thought. He closed the canopy door.

For a moment, Hu considered dousing the flame, taking the hose from the doorway and sealing himself in, but it was no good.

Even with the wind shut outside Hu knew he'd be dead by morning.

He turned back to his foot, which was growing colder on the canopy floor. Once again he worked it. He sat forward to do this and felt something hard in the pocket of his aviator's jacket.

The magazine!

A small flame of hope kindled in his mind's eye and just as quickly went dead. I don't know where that bitch left my gun, he thought bitterly. It was too dark and too cold to go ranging around for the AK now.

Hu picked up the surgical gauze and began winding it around his feet. He had hung the wet sock on the wire chair frame and it was now completely dry. Hu tied off the gauze and put on his sock while thinking of Mun.

True, the security chief's daughter was more trouble than she was worth, but he wished no harm to come to her.

Hu knew, however, that Mun had failed to leave the vault for a very good reason. He hoped she wasn't dead.

The animal noise came through the crack at the canopy door again. It was answered by another and another.

Hu picked up the K-bar and hunched before the fire with his legs splayed to either side of the heat source. The K-bar rested blade up, cupped in both hands, which rested in his lap. Hu's face had become very still and serious but when he looked down at the knife he grinned.

Sex was the furthest thing from his mind.

MUN GIYANG CRIED INTO THE SNOW long after the slab of rock had closed on her. Then she slept.

When she came to again, the pain in her back was less the pain of a knife being twisted. It was more like the pain of being hit by a club. Dull was not the word she would use to describe it, Mun thought, but it no longer screamed at her.

She was disgusted with herself for failing to escape, for being weak and vulnerable. She was the kind of person who was afraid of facing her limitations. She had been a spoiled and lonely kid whose attitude toward failure and weakness was simply contempt.

Mun wasn't very generous. In the past, she never *had* to be that way. Now, when accidental failure entered her life with the sudden decisiveness of the rock being lowered, Mun was not able to be generous again, not even with herself.

She just didn't know how.

What she did know was the difference between a game cock and a quitter....

Mun rolled onto her side. She could still feel the result of the clubbing but she was game. Propped on her right elbow, Mun dug into her coat pocket. Matches, she thought.

Her hand came away full of matches and cigarettes, a pack of Virginia Slims, her last from the four cartons she'd bought in New York.

Her gloved hands shook when she tried to light the smoke. She yelled the Mandarin word for "shit" loudly into the dark cave and threw the cigarette and the match down the slope at her feet.

Mun rolled onto her back, letting her elbows prop her up so her bad side, her hurt side, would have no contact with the cold ground. She fumbled for the cigarettes again and this time lit one.

No tobacco had ever tasted so good.

Mun held the match up and looked around her. Clearly she was right at the mouth of Kanamuto's vault. The long shadows inside the door shook as moving air touched her match. Mun smelled the singed wool of her glove and tossed the tiny flame into the hole.

She had seen the crates before. Before the darkness returned she saw them again. There were many more than she'd expected.

Mun took out another match and moved down the tunnel toward the first of the crates.

It looked as if it would make a good fire....

STRASSKO DREAMED OF A BRIGHT LIGHT—the brightest fire he had ever imagined burned in his dream. It was as brilliant as the sun and it was surrounded by darkness.

When he woke up, Strassko's eyes hurt with the memory of the dream.

He looked at his watch. It was exactly dawn. From the window of the Chinese hut, Strassko could see the truck with which he'd transported Dr. Kanamuto's crate. No one was else was visible.

Strassko's head ached slightly, maybe from the dream, maybe from the vodka. He'd been a fool to drink so much last night, but the vodka had set his mind free to roam the contours of the big map.

He had not found what he was looking for. The surface held no telltale trace of a cave entrance, at least not as far as he could see.

Still, Strassko was now completely familiar with the territory of his search. He knew what to expect and where the most likely areas were located.

It would be hard, he decided, not only because Kanamuto had blown the damn entrance all those years ago. There was also enough snow on the ground to hide the average-sized car.

And, Strassko thought, my head feels as though it were lined with sandpaper. He stretched.

There was a bowl of far-gone fruit on a side table near the door. As he was leaving, Strassko grabbed it in his left hand.

A glance back at the desk reminded him that he'd left the map. That was all right. Let Strakhov think he was no longer interested in germs or China.

Strassko knew how to stretch his edge.

He flipped the door open and walked into the subzero air, sensing that the truck would not start first thing. It was too cold, far too cold.

From a toolbox, Strassko withdrew a length of rubber hose. He used it to suck a quantity of gas from the tank. Then he primed the carb. As he'd expected, the truck started immediately.

Strassko shut the hood and hung the hose from the radio on the dash. He had already decided to start his search at the Japanese Imperial Testing Facility, a mound of rubble covered in three feet of snow.

THE HARBIN MOUNTAIN ROAD was no superhighway. There were no white lines and reflectors anywhere in China. It was also dark, and snow was blowing in the cab with vicious persistence.

Bolan had gained some distance on the one remaining truck simply by hiding directly over the lip of a steep hill with the truck in neutral and his foot on the brake.

When the Chinese vehicle came over the hill after him, he braced himself and released the brake.

It was a shock. Sure. But at first the Chinese were too startled to shoot. The collision sent him rolling down the hill in neutral, fighting to control the empty vehicle on the road.

The truck behind was less lucky, however. Its radiator was crushed and it made the shoulder only by accident before the last truck could crash into it.

The last truck stopped to take on the men from the first. No one was eager to be left alone in the hills on this kind of night.

After that incident, the Chinese came over each hill cautiously. The Executioner just sailed on through. The snow streaming through the windshield didn't help any, but after putting some miles between himself and his pursuers, Bolan relaxed a little.

There was a funny side to the way things were taking place, and the big man was quick to appreciate the weird situation. The snow came through the windshield in big gobs as he slammed through the night, but the high beams cut the murk and the wide span of the workmanlike axles held the vehicle to the road.

Bolan even laughed a little when he started getting into it. He'd have to put it down somewhere and wait for the morning, but meanwhile he was enjoying his freedom after being cooped up at sea and in the crate.

Just as he was thinking about putting it down, he saw the light. He couldn't be sure at first. Every time he looked he got wet snow in his right eye. That was the side the light was on.

There it was again.

Through the gaps in the continuously moving curtain of snow Bolan's eyes centered on a light. It was roughly ahead in the direction the road was taking, and he made for it with renewed speed.

He had no idea how far behind the Chinese were but a light's a light, he decided.

When the road curved he passed within a half mile of it. It was on his left now. Bolan pulled far enough off the road that the headlights of the army truck following him would miss him.

He killed the motor and began walking toward the shack.

He wondered if its occupant had heard his approach.

HU CAME AWAKE with a start and realized he was drooling.

He was hunched over inside the sleeping bag with his head almost between his parted legs. There was a noise outside again that sent him scrambling for the K-bar.

It was the wolves.

Hu's breath came in short gasps, and a feeling of disbelief sped through his body as he grabbed at the wire frame of the chair for his boots.

They were dry. Hu noticed the fire had burned low but he had no time. He stuffed his feet into the boots, feeling the pain in his toes. A bad sign, he knew. But there was no time.

The fire burned low. It was all coals now, resting on the ash-tinted stones that filled the bottom of his makeshift fireplace. Hu rolled on his side and brushed the sleeping sack away from his chest.

He leaned on his right arm and pulled the chimney tube from the upper corner of the door. There was barely any smoke now. A thin line of it trailed out of the tube as Hu flung it behind him.

Now Hu leaned forward, reaching toward the underside of the left door with his left hand. It was free from obstructions, and he meant to secure it against the wolves.

It would be cold in the canopy, but he knew he would rather freeze than face hungry wolves.

Before he touched the door, he remembered to pick up the K-bar. It was good move, a smart one, but at the time Hu was not thinking—he was moving.

He put his hand out of the canopy to seal himself inside. His fingers had barely closed around the isinglass when a hot bayonet seared into his arm. Hu screamed.

It was not one bayonet, it was many.

The locked jaw of a Siberian wolf tugged at his arm, pulling him half out of the door. Hu's head spilled over the rim of the canopy. He was looking sideways into the teeth and eyes of an animal the size of a Shetland pony, and the thing still had him in its jaws.

Hu swung the K-bar overhand. He heard the blade scrape the isinglass surface and push the door out at the wolf. He brought the knife down hard onto the animal's skull, feeling the good steel bite into the hellhound's head over the left eye.

The thing made an unusual sound then. It had been snarling like a wind out of Russia. When the knife bit into it, the snarl wound down as the breath escaped the dead-but-still-standing animal. It collapsed slowly. Its jaws were still locked around Hu's arm.

Hu's hand remained gripped around the knife. It came away bloody from the wolf's head, and Hu would have continued to lie half in and half out of the cockpit if the canopy door had not been struck by another body, another wolf snarling now and snapping its jaws toward Hu's throat.

The second wolf leaped toward Hu. Its shoulder struck the canopy and slammed it into Hu's shoulder. Hu dropped the knife even as the jaws snapped a half inch away from his neck. "Whoa-ho!" Hu cried as he snapped back inside the chopper.

The canopy door slammed shut behind him.

He was safe but he was wounded. He had no fire. He had no knife. His feet were all but useless. Outside, the wolf snarled and struck at the door with his jaw.

Behind him Hu heard a second snarl.

10

The muzzle of the big handgun pressed into the wiry old man's neck suddenly, but he did not leap away in surprise. Instead he turned to confront the intruder.

"I heard your truck," he said. "You thought I didn't." He spoke Russian naturally. Bolan noted that the man had taken in the Executioner's Soviet uniform without a specific glance.

"Who are you?" Bolan asked.

"I am the geologist Shu." He brushed the gun away from his neck casually. "Please," he said. "Sit. You're welcome here."

"Turn out the lights," Bolan ordered. He put the backpack down beside the cushion he had chosen on the floor. Shu looked impassively at the insignia on the bag. His face was emotionless, but he looked straight into the Executioner's soul.

"How many are following you?" he asked.

"One truck. At least eight men."

"Are they the army?" he asked, then caught himself. "They must be the army if they have a truck. Do they know you have that?" He nodded at Bolan's bag.

The Executioner nodded slightly.

Shu frowned, worried, but doused the kerosene lamp that illuminated the small room. "You are interested in the germs," he told Bolan flatly.

The Executioner was stunned. He had been holding the AutoMag loosely, but now his grip tightened on the butt. "Start talking," he growled at the frail older man.

"I am the government's geologist," Shu said. "But I will not allow anyone to have those germs." A dark cloud passed over his face as he spoke.

"I don't want them," Bolan said.

"What is your intention?"

"The way I see it," Bolan said, fitting the Magnum back into his shoulder rig, "the only good thing about those bugs is that they're contained."

Shu nodded. "Correct. They can be destroyed more easily that way."

"So," Bolan continued, "I'm going to find the caves. I'm going to find the germs and I'm going to blow them up with that." He gestured toward the backpack.

"What is your name?" Shu asked pleasantly. He was standing in the darkness beside the wood stove. Now he poured a cup of hot tea, allowed it to cool and handed it to Bolan. The Executioner could barely make out its shape in the semidarkness, but the orange shades of the fire caught his hand as he moved toward it.

The cup was hot and welcome.

"I'm called Bolan," Bolan said.

"Are you Russian?"

"No." He hesitated. "I, uh, I sort of work independently."

"That is often necessary," Shu said. He moved across the room and gestured toward a stack of boxes in the far corner. They were covered in a tarp, which he pulled away.

"I don't suppose you can read Chinese?"

Bolan nodded, then spoke. "No."

"This says dynamite," Shu told him. He was pointing toward one of the boxes but even with his exceptional night vision the Executioner could see nothing. He said so.

"I was forgetting," Shu told him. "I have spent my life studying caves. My eyes need very little light."

"You were going to blow up the germs?" Bolan asked.

"I was going to blow up the tunnel in which the germs are located," Shu told him, explaining about the natural gas.

"You see, once the gas explodes the entire network of caves will become a furnace. Even if Kanamuto has hidden other caches of the viruses in other tunnels, it will all be destroyed."

"You've got a lot of dynamite," Bolan said appreciatively.

Shu smiled. "Fortunately, it is no longer necessary. I am an old man," he explained. "It would take me days to carry all this into the cave."

"It's nearby?" Bolan couldn't believe his luck.

"The Wah-ling entrance is three-quarters of the way up the hill behind this shack."

Bolan nodded, finally allowing himself to relax. "Show me tomorrow," he said. The good news brought with it a desire to sleep.

Over the storm noise outside, Bolan heard a truck.

His right hand reached for the AutoMag as he stood up in the dark. With his left he picked up the backpack.

"Come," Shu said. "It is an easy climb. Even for an old man."

The Executioner realized that there would be no sleep tonight.

THE TORCH SHE'D MADE CRACKLED AND POPPED when the rags torn from her blouse burned down to the wood. Mun was now naked under her coat. Her firm breasts brushed the sheepskin lining as she turned back and forth stiffly. She was examining each case.

On the floor behind her were three more torches. When they were gone, Mun knew she could burn more crates.

As she lifted the lid of one with her left hand, the pain once again caught her in the kidney. She cried out and dropped it, holding on to the top of the crate momentarily until she could recover.

Then Mun straightened and passed the torch to her left hand.

With her right now free, she once again opened the lid and peered inside.

Row after row of stainless-steel vacuum bottles lined the shelves of each padded crate. Mun selected the nearest bottle and gripped it under her left elbow while she forced the lid off.

She withdrew a corked bakelite test tube filled with liquid that was alternately brown then orange under the flickering torch.

It didn't look like much, Mun admitted, but within each test tube there were enough bacilli to cause an epidemic in a major city.

There were at least twenty crates.

Mun returned the test tube and vacuum bottle to their resting place and set down the lid gingerly. Her Japanese was very poor, but she recognized a few of them on this particular crate.

"Russian subjects only," it read.

Mun knew that the other crates would contain bacilli for white *and* black Americans as well as Chinese.

When she looked up, Mun noticed that her torch flickered in an air current that ran away from the sealed vault entrance.

Her hopes soared. Feeling that she had discovered a way out, Mun hurried down the length of the vault. But when she came within sight of a mound of rubble she realized she was truly trapped.

Still, the air current was stronger at the rubble's base. Mun set her torch in a gap in the stones and set about building a fire.

When I get warm, I might be able to dig through this mess, she thought. There was a gap of a few inches near the top of the pile. She knew she'd never be able to reach it. The pain in her side was too intense.

Mun pushed her fear into the back of her mind and separated the lid from the nearest crate. After she broke it with a rock she noticed one of the shards was long and strong enough to use as a lever.

THE NIGHT WAS WILD AROUND THEM. Snow whirled in eddies off the rock face as Bolan and Shu picked their way up the hill.

The old man had said it was an easy walk, but it was not. The earth and stone under their feet was treacherous in the snow. The air was freezing, and they were constantly pushed right and left on the narrow trail as the blizzard raged around them.

Bolan's progress was quicker than the old man's in the steepest passages. At one point he caught the left arm of the winded geologist and half-carried him up the slope.

They reached a plateau, and Shu told him that there was not much farther to go. He rested, puffing and wheezing, but still he was game for someone his age.

Bolan guessed the man to be sixty-five.

He turned back toward the shack, searching the white-black night for some sign of the soldiers.

"Are they far behind?" Shu wondered.

Bolan shrugged. It was impossible to tell in this night. He turned up his collar and jerked his head toward the slope. It was time to push on.

Shu was leaning over with his hands on his knees, but when he saw the Executioner's gesture he nodded. Reluctantly.

Shu straightened, but before he could move he caught a gust of snow from an eddy full in the face. Bolan watched the humor and surprise work their way over the old man's face. The geologist opened his mouth to laugh but caught himself in time.

That was smart, the Executioner thought appreciatively. Smart and fast. "Think you could have carried all that high explosive up here?" he asked the old man.

Shu nodded. "But it would have taken me a week," he said.

They came to the lip of the cave after another half hour's ascent.

Shu entered immediately. Bolan soon lost track of his shape as it was engulfed by the dark, open mouth.

He turned away from the entrance and strained his senses to catch whatever was down the hillside behind them. He needed to know how far behind the soldiers were.

There was a chance, a slim one Bolan knew, that the storm would obscure their footprints before the soldiers could find them.

Shu appeared behind him suddenly, wearing a miner's hat with a light attached to the front peak. He handed a similar one to Bolan. "Come," Shu told him. "It's warmer inside."

Bolan wondered how warm it could be in an ice cave. He flicked on the lamp on the helmet after they entered and discovered that it was warmer.

"As we descend," Shu said, "it will get mercilessly cold."

"How far in are we going?" Bolan asked.

"Five hours. When we get to the base of the Grand Shu Ravine—" Shu smiled at the mention of his own name "—when we get there," he continued, "we are at the closest point to the natural gas. Detonate there and the whole place will light up."

Bolan nodded and slipped the backpack onto his right shoulder. He had a long night ahead of him, he decided, trying not to think of the soldiers.

After that, there would be another long day.

HU SAT MOTIONLESS in the cold air of the helicopter. He stared straight ahead. His features, even his eyes, were motionless but his mind raced.

Once again he gripped the K-bar in both hands, but this time they were covered with blood from the wolf and the man.

Outside Hu could see the head of the wolf as it tried to gnaw its way through the isinglass. Its teeth slid off the frosted surface, and its muzzle rubbed sideways in Hu's direction as the beast tried to gain a purchase with its teeth.

Feeling something like humor, Hu picked up the bottle of iodine and poured it through the crack in the door. The smell would have been enough to buy him a short respite, but the wolf actually gummed some and for a moment made a comical face that raised Hu's drained spirits.

Then it attacked again.

The iodine had just made it mad. It rammed into the canopy door with a force that rocked the helicopter and moved it. Hu felt the remaining iodine slop accidently onto his wounded arm. He ignored the pain and reversed the bottle.

Now he held it upside down like a beer bottle in a bar-fighter's fist. He picked up the K-bar again, thinking about the next move. The second wolf had joined the first at the canopy door. They showed no sign of getting tired.

Hu was cold. The fire in the medical box had burned down so long ago. A few glowing embers remained, but Hu knew he could not use any of the wood. The small space would fill up with smoke immediately and force him into the open.

Suddenly he had a thought! The problem was that if he remained *inside* he would freeze, choke or get eaten. But Hu thought he might have a chance if he went *outside*.

Hu banked the firebox and used sticks to push it across the floor to the wolf-covered door. Then he rolled up his space-blanket sleeping bag and stuffed it inside the aviator jacket.

He propped the wire chair frame against the door and levered one corner of the firebox onto it. When Hu withdrew the stick, the firebox rested unstably in front of the doorjamb.

Then he slopped the remaining alcohol across the floor. He stood painfully and unlatched the door farthest from the wolves. He took a stick and unlatched the wolf-side door.

Both timber wolves snarled on the other side of the space-blanket curtain. The noise had set them off again.

He could see patches of fur and the animals' backs out the small crack in the curtain. He braced himself, then shoved the door open toward the wolves.

As Hu shoved, he jumped. He was outside again and for a moment the sharp, cold air felt good. Wonderful! Then he landed.

The pain in his feet shot up his legs. Hu didn't like it but he could stand it. He heard the canopy door spring back behind him and he hobbled around the front of the helicopter, smashing his stick against the far door to close it.

The fire was gathering inside. The second and smaller of the wolves had caught a rear leg in the door and turned back toward it, yelping as the fire came up. Hu smashed his stick at the leg and door and drove the frightened animal back into the cabin, into the fire.

Hu beat on the door and it snapped shut.

Now I wait, Hu thought.

He pulled the space blanket from his jacket and set it in the soft snow. The howling of the wolves bothered him not a bit. He had seen what packs of hungry wolves could do to a man. He would never let that happen to him.

Hu settled into the space blanket. When he leaned back into the snow he felt something brush his back. He turned to it. It was the AK!

Hu moved quickly, despite his sensationless feet. He snapped the butt end of the mechanism against the canopy. He struggled with his numb fingers to get to the magazine in his pocket. He loaded it and set the weapon for auto-fire.

The howls of the wolves were becoming more human, more ragged and pitiful. Hu had been prepared to listen to them as long as that was the only way to survive but now that he had firepower the sounds were going to stop.

He steadied himself in front of the door. He sent a mad burst over the canopy, then he snapped open the door and swung to the side as the heat poured out at him.

Hu was firing across the canopy. The smaller wolf's head shot out toward him as he fired. It was burning. The skin had peeled back on one side. Hu's bile rose as he saw it. It was easy to kill.

The second wolf was still burning. Hu poured a burst into its heaving diaphragm and the dead thing keeled into the flame, hissing and crackling. It was over. But Hu's shelter was burning.

The top of the canopy had not yet broken open or into flame but the plastic was a molten yellow brown and in the center it was black.

Hu heaped snow into the burning chopper and pushed at the far door with his weapon. When the catch came free on the door, Hu forced as much of the burning matter out as he could.

He grabbed the closest wolf, the smaller one. It lay across the opening. Hu heaved the carcass out behind him. Then he brushed the burning material away and grabbed the second wolf.

When the carcass cleared the door this time, he was left with wolf hair and debris across his jacket. It stank.

He was not enjoying this. The flying snow was also an irritant.

When Hu had cleared the fire from his shelter, he waited while the heat inside burned off the moisture. The top of the canopy had finally broken and gusts of steam from the melted snow poured out into the swirling air.

At least he wouldn't have to worry about another chimney, he thought. He checked the debris. There was still enough unburned matter for him to survive the night, but now Hu's arm was bothering him.

He could endure the pain and he knew that the wolf had not found an artery, but he worried about the exposed flesh in this cold.

He knew he would not be able to walk free of this mess. His feet were soaked through now from the wet snow. They were completely without feeling and Hu knew he would not be able to walk one kilometer, let alone ten!

He turned toward the radio. It was a scorched cinder.

Now Hu was reduced to waiting for help. It was not a feeling he enjoyed.

He looked disgustedly at the wolves' bodies, wondering if he would be forced to eat them.

Life, which *had* seemed so good in the moments when he was overcoming the wolves, was now bitter.

With the thought of bitterness still in his mind, the good pilot, Hu, took his last piece of Pear Tree gum from his jacket pocket and set to work.

11

Vesh knew it was morning. He had watched the light come up through the tiny slit of a window.

Vesh was in a long narrow room with concrete walls, a steel door and a cot on which he now rested.

His hands were shackled to the wall behind him, and the position made Vesh feel like a holy martyr.

He had not slept all night. The desperateness of his position churned in his gut the way small, sharp stones churn in an eddy. His eyes were bloodshot and his nerves were jangled but he knew he had an ace in the hole.

He could feel it nestling inside his boot.

If Strakhov made the tiniest slip, the sailor knew he'd catch it and use it.

I might die today, the sailor thought worriedly.

Still, there was a part of him that still grinned.

I might not, this part said. Vesh liked this part. Courage was new to him. He knew something had grown inside him since yesterday when he bluffed Strakhov. It was something good, Vesh thought in surprise.

He knew it would also be something useful.

He heard footsteps heading toward him along the corridor and braced himself for the beginning of this day. It *will* be my day either way, Vesh decided.

He knew it no longer mattered whether he lived or died today. Vesh Slovincik was learning to live large.

The door opened and General Greb Strakhov entered. He looked drawn and worried. It comforted the Yugoslav to know that Strakhov, too, had had a bad night.

He decided to push it, to tax the man. Maybe that way the general would be more likely to slip up. Vesh waited until the man was close to his cot.

"Do you know," he asked conversationally, "what Marshal Tito used to say was the difference between a Russian woman and a Russian soldier?"

The cruel line of Strakhov's mouth drew back in a grimace of surprise.

"Marshal Tito said," Vesh told him, "a Russian woman has balls."

ALTHOUGH STRASSKO HAD NEVER visited China, the ruins of the Japanese Imperial Testing Facility were easy enough to find. The shortage of vehicles and fuel in the Asian giant and the lack of personal freedoms made traveling a luxury. China didn't have many roads. Harbin had only two.

Strassko was on the only northeasterly route now. He'd checked the map before coming to the airport and seen that he would have to take a left. The road had led him past the Kai-bin cave entrance where he knew Strakhov planned to search for the germs.

Now, however, he was descending out of the hills north of Kai-bin. As he geared down the hill, Strassko made out the snow-covered ruins of what had been a warehouse structure.

It was less than two kilometers away.

Strassko could see something else, too.

Less than half a kilometer from the ruins was another kind of ruin. Strassko strained at the frosted window and made out what seemed to be the recent wreck of a helicopter, stranded in the ravine he would have to cross to get to Kanamuto's facility.

Strassko strained harder. He licked the edge of his right hand and rubbed a small patch of the frost completely clear in his field of vision. He mopped up the moisture with his elbow automatically and was left with a small crystalline patch in the middle of the smoky glass.

Russians, Strassko thought, know how to drive in winter.

Before him he could see the helicopter more clearly. The extent of the damage to it, especially to the canopy, was horrendous.

No one could have survived such a blast.

Strassko had never seen such a destroyed vehicle. He had seen helicopters that had been blown up by rockets. The effect had been just as impressive.

When hand-held rockets struck a chopper as small as this the most they would leave was a skeleton like that of some dead insect.

This wreck, however, looked as if it had burned from the inside. Part of him wondered what had caused it, but mainly he was interested in another aspect of the broken bird.

Before it, where everything else was covered in snow, there lay a huge slab of partly exposed rock.

Attached to the rock was a cable that ran to the underbelly of the wreck.

Strassko noticed something else in the snow beside the smoking canopy. Three child-sized mounds lay at awkward angles to the canopy door.

Strassko knew they were wolves. Patches of wolf fur broke through the wind-blasted holes in each mound.

Something is strange here, he thought. But his mind returned to the large rock slab.

Now he was very close to it. Beneath the snow he could see the outlines of other bits of debris. They looked much like the ruins of the testing facility had looked as he'd driven down from the hills. Strassko exulted. This was it.

He pulled to within a dozen meters of the rock slab. He was now above it, with the radiator pointed toward the rock, the helicopter and, far beyond them, the testing facility.

Strassko knew that some enterprising soldier had found the prize before him but it did not matter.

The other person had obviously failed.

He suspected that one had developed some exotic kind of engine failure when the rock placed its incredible strain on the bird's little motor. Power pack trouble, maybe, or a burst fuel line. Strassko knew nothing about engines.

It didn't matter what had happened, however. Strassko was definitely pleased *something* had gone wrong.

He exited the cab, resisting the urge to investigate the disaster at the chopper. He would find out the why and how after he held the what in his hands.

The Russian leaned in front of the grill and flicked a switch at the bumper. Then he began to pull a steel cable down the slope toward the slab of rock.

It suddenly crossed his mind that once he had the germs, he would be free to use Shu's fastburn....

...While Strakhov was in the caves...!

Strassko's feet tripped lightly down the slippery slope. He felt like a man who had won it all and beaten everyone.

There was Shu, he thought, an ineffectual academic, more interested in preserving peace and having his name on a forgotten geographical feature than he was in practical things like power and money.

Strassko laughed. Then there was Ling, the embittered spy chief of a third-rate service, forced to cooperate with his mortal enemies. An insipid man, really, he thought. Unworthy.

There was also the mad American, the man driven mad by a desire for revenge that he ennobled with a different name. Strassko knew that Mack Bolan was just another desperate bloodhound hell-bent on revenge. A dishonest bloodhound at that, he thought.

The man is weak! He had to excuse his need for revenge by using a fancy word. He had to call it justice.

Lastly, and Strassko savored this, there was the *dreaded* Major-General Strakhov, hero of Leningrad, Guderion's equal.

This, he knew, was best of all.

Sergei Strassko had beaten Strakhov!

Today I will kill him, he thought.

It was almost February. The bright winter sun glinted off the new snow with an intensity that would have hurt his eyes at any other moment.

But at this moment, this *moment of moments*, Strassko felt bathed in light. He felt like singing. Really.

I feel like singing, Strassko told himself. He was about to, but he stopped, suddenly feeling a little foolish.

His pride won out, though. "If I feel like singing," Sergei Strassko said aloud to the Chinese wilderness, "I will sing...."

He began to fasten the cable to the rock slab. The song was about what the housewives of Brest like to do when their husbands go to war.

It was a happy song. Sergei Strassko was happy.

Behind him in the burned-out helicopter, something living, barely living, stirred. If Strassko had been looking in that direction, he might have noticed the wreck tilt slightly on its skids or seen a patch of snow drop from the rotor that bobbed briefly with the movement inside.

Strassko saw nothing. He was running back up the slope toward the winch....

INSIDE THE SOVIET GENERAL'S QUARTERS, the crate labeled Machine Parts had once again been sealed.

Ling stood in the doorway, a slight, small man. Han the driver hovered behind.

Ling cast his quick, dark eyes around the interior of the room. There was something wrong here, an odor that was wrong.

Ling noticed that many small chafing dishes had been placed around the room. They were filled with colorless liquid.

He dipped his finger in one and touched the droplet to his lips.

Vinegar. Ling knew it was an old way to get rid of the stink of putrification in the desperate conditions of field hospitals.

Leningrad, he thought.

Ling walked into the room and motioned Han to open the crate.

The young man gasped audibly when he uncovered the fetid corpse. Ling nodded grimly.

"He died in transit?"

Han shook his head and the desperation in his face showed. "What will we do?" he asked. "What if the Soviets get the germs and shut us out completely?"

Ling considered this.

"Their only transport is still on the runway. We will go to Harbin airport and wait for Strakhov there." As he said it, Ling regretted taking this last course. He knew he had lost the advantages of mobility and initiative. But it was out of his hands.

"Airport," he ordered, brushing past Han on his way to the car. "Seal the borders," he snapped. The young man scrambled to the radio.

"Seal the caves," Ling added as an afterthought. "Seal it all."

"Do you hear that?" Shu asked him. The glow of the other man's light turned on the floor in front of him.

Bolan turned back to Shu. They stood in the darkness of the cave, hearing the air move through the immense cavity.

It was like a silence, but it was an active silence.

Faintly, in the direction from which they had come, they heard a regular noise, like something brushing rock.

"Footsteps," Shu said. "A half hour behind. They have not yet reached the ravine. Your soldiers?"

Bolan nodded.

"Then we may not leave here alive," Shu said. "I did not really expect them to be stupid enough to follow us in."

Bolan grinned. "Look," he said, "you double back. There's no point in..."

Shu touched his arm in the dark. His grip was firm. "You need me to guide you to the vault. This is also *my* victory, Comrade Bo-lan."

"Will they be able to see our lights?" the Executioner asked.

"By the time we reach the Shu ravine," Shu said, "they will be able to see us sporadically. The surface of these walls is very irregular. We will be out of their sight much of the time."

"How about our range?" Bolan asked.

"We will be out of range until the trip back," Shu told him. "If we are lucky, we can climb up the other side of the ravine."

"We'll have to leave those guys in here to die if we make it," Bolan told him. He looked at the old man's face. Shu nodded.

"The only certainty is that the germs will be destroyed," Shu said. "There is a very good chance we will all die."

Bolan liked what he saw in the old man's eyes. There was compassion, sure. Hell, the Executioner also didn't like the idea of killing guys who were basically on his side.

It must have been harder for Shu. But there was cold determination in the geologist's face. "We cannot let anyone get hold of Dr. Kanamuto's evil," he said simply. "I have known that all along."

"How'd you find 'em in the first place?" the Executioner wondered.

"I found them when I was doing a recent report for our government," Shu said. "There were five choices of caves. I picked the most obvious and followed it. They were right there."

"What about the report?"

"I lied," Shu said. "Please do not tell anyone." They laughed together. For the first time since Brooklyn the Executioner's burden was lifted. He stood straight and tall in the semidarkness, shouldering the backpack and its deadly contents with the ease of a man carrying a child at a picnic.

"And the fastburn will *definitely* work?" Bolan half asked, half stated.

Shu nodded and pursed his lips, "It is a sure thing. It could be repeated anywhere by anyone. All you need is the gas, the explosion and a network of unobstructed caves."

"Unobstructed?"

"Not blocked by rockfalls and such," Shu told him. "Don't worry, Comrade Bo-lan. That could never happen here."

"MOVE, FOOL." Strakhov pushed the man through the mouth of the cave. They were completely alone. Vesh was handcuffed with his wrists behind his back. He was spending most of his time wondering how long it would take him to get the palm gun out of his boot.

He had never been very agile, and his fat belly would prevent him from leaning backward with any ease.

It will probably take me as much as half a minute to get the damn thing into my hand and straighten up, Vesh thought.

Then I have to shoot the bastard.

That last part was going to be really tricky. Vesh would have to fire his pistol upside down and backward.

I will have to do it in parts, he decided. First, I'll get the gun when he's not watching me. A very tall order, he told himself skeptically. Then, he continued, *then* I wait. I press up close to him when it is natural to do it, maybe in a tight part of the cave, he thought.

When I get him close enough, I'll shoot.

He didn't expect to kill the man on his first try.

But he did want to kill him.

Kill him and get away.

He was having so much fun thinking about this, Vesh forgot the pain in his nose.

Caked blood spread in a V across his upper lip. He had to breathe through his mouth now, and when he did the blood at the corners cracked and rasped.

Strakhov hadn't liked the sailor's little joke.

What do I care? Vesh Slovincik told himself. That ugly Soviet prick is as good as dead.

12

Incredibly the rock lifted.

Strassko knew nothing about motors, so he didn't know to be surprised that the truck's winch could tug the light far end of the rock slab free and clear of the vault.

Strassko waited until the rock was nearly perpendicular before he shut down the winch.

He was down the slope at breakneck speed, anxious to see the cave that no one had seen for forty years. Strassko stood at the opening, searching the vault before he entered.

Something was strange.

It was not as dark as it should have been.

There was also the smell of burning wood. Strassko's eyes became wild.

What if someone *has* been here first? What if someone had burned his precious germs?

He could think of no other reason for the odor of wood smoke. From inside the side pocket of his woolen coat, Strassko withdrew a Tokarev TT 33, an old-style Soviet assassin's weapon from the Omnipool armories, a personal favorite of Sergei Strassko.

He moved forward down Kanamuto's wrecked slope.

Yes. There was light inside the cave. Light and fire.

Strassko stood in the opening of the cave silhouetted against the dull winter light from outside. As his eyes be came accustomed to the semidarkness, he noticed three things.

There were wooden crates with Japanese characters on them.

Strassko's heart pounded with excitement.

Some of the crates had been broken open and the contents disturbed.

Strassko became suspicious.

At the far end of the gallery, a dark figure rested beside a fire that supplied the only light in the cave.

For the longest moment in his life Strassko looked into the unyielding blackness at the figure beside the fire. He gave the figure a face. He gave the figure a name.

The skin on the Soviet's scalp tingled. It was him! How could he be here?

How had he been in Montreal? In Brooklyn? In Vladivostok?

How had he killed Demeter and cheated Strakhov out of Kanamuto's treasure?

Sergei Strassko looked at the black figure resting beside the fire and knew that he had badly underestimated the Executioner. He raised the Tokarev to fire, but his eyes had adjusted now.

The flames licked around the broken wood and cast triangles of light on the seated figure, making it look like a bizarre harlequin in black and orange.

It was a girl! It was not Mack Bolan. It was just a girl.

Strassko advanced on her, feeling powerful and released from his fear but angry at himself for being afraid.

He had looked so real. Strassko would have sworn he'd seen the Executioner sitting there waiting for him.

He reached Mun now. She could see the cruel lines of hate stretch from his nose and contort his lips into a grimace.

Strassko smashed her across the face with the back of his left hand. His right hand held the Tokarev close to her face.

Who is this bitch, he thought.

He knew that Mun had seen his fear.

She turned back to him with a cold expression of absolute disgust. There was blood on her lip. He liked that. She was quite beautiful. He had always liked Oriental women.

Strassko reached toward her chin. He caressed her briefly but Mun pulled her face out of the man's hand and sneered at him wordlessly. Strassko struck her across the base of her neck with the Tokarev's barrel.

She gasped but did not cry out.

She is a bitch, Strassko thought. Everything else had gone out of his mind. He was safe in this place. He knew it.

There was no one for miles. He had the lead on everyone. He could take his pleasure with this girl *and* have the germs *and* kill Strakhov.

Who would stop him?

Strassko's eyes looked like the eyes of a snake. Hooded. Dispassionate. Predatory. He grabbed her chin and forced her to look at him. He ran the barrel of the Tokarev across the bruise on her neck.

She pulled away. Her face was set. She had not allowed him to see the pain that he knew the bruise had caused her. He grabbed a handful of her black, silken hair and forced her head back until she was staring up at him.

Then he ran the Tokarev's barrel down the V of her coat, tugging the fabric away until the lush white flesh of her breasts was exposed to him and his breath came in short gusts.

Was she ashamed? Was she humiliated? Strassko wanted to see it on her face.

Again he tugged back her head by the hair, giving her a snake look. She was strong. Even Strassko had to admit to that. She showed nothing. No fear.

He liked that.

It made him hot.

"I am called Strakhov," he said. He rubbed the cold barrel of the assassin's weapon against her cheek. He liked the way her black eyes glinted in the firelight beside her.

AT THIS POINT THE LEDGE NARROWED. He was walking head down now, training his eyes on the path before him, spreading his antennae into the far corners of the cave to compensate for the limited use of his eyes.

Then Mack Bolan heard a shot. A plok, really. Something like a .38 in a weird gun. It was far away. He couldn't be sure of the direction, but it sounded as if it came from behind and to the left.

Bolan turned. As he turned, he heard the auto-fire behind them. Shu pitched forward with a look of surprise on his face.

His miner's helmet rolled free. Bolan tried to kick it back from the edge, but it rolled on its rim and pitched over the side.

Shu's breath came in short gasps. Bolan heard his "unh-unh" noises beside his ear, but he could not take his eyes off the light of the miner's helmet as it winked on and off, spinning down the bottomless ravine.

An air current must have caught it. It surged upward, a small light hardly visible, like a white lie in the middle of a horrible black truth.

The auto-fire came in again, sighting on Bolan's helmet. He grabbed Shu's shoulders and forced the wounded man back against the rock.

The contact must have hurt Shu. He yelled and winced.

Bolan was having a hard time keeping a grip on the narrow ledge. He felt the bullets impact on the rock above his head and knew that the PLA soldiers were on to him. He turned away to give them nothing to shoot at.

Now his light pointed down the trail. Shu was safe for the moment. Bolan freed his hand and shut off his own.

The silence came down like the darkness.

Shu was beside him in the darkness. In the complete, absolute black of the cave, things took on a radical edge. There were no outlines. Things had no reality.

Beside him Shu wheezed.

"I will not be able to lead you out of here, Comrade Bolan."

"Don't talk. You'll make it worse."

"It is the..." Shu searched for a Russian word. "It is the lungs."

Bolan grimaced. A sucking wound.

"Can you get me to the spot?" It was a hard question. In different circumstances, it would have been a very cruel question, but Shu understood.

Bolan had known that Shu would understand. They were both in this now. They had been all along.

Shu understood that Bolan was not using him so that the Executioner could live. Shu's death was just a matter of time, but so was Bolan's.

The Executioner's numbers were clearly falling. They had to deploy the fastburn before Strakhov or Ling or whoever got to the vault before them.

Shu knew Bolan would arm the bomb *even if* there was no way out. Bolan heard an intake of breath.

"I can get you there," Shu said.

"I know you will, buddy," Bolan told the man in English. He picked up the geologist in his arms and carried him like a child down the slope of the Grand Shu Ravine toward death.

HU HAD HEARD THE MAN'S SINGING in his stupor and wondered where the hell a Russian would come from in the middle of this Chinese wasteland.

Then he remembered the germs. His skin began to crawl.

Hu leaned forward stiffly and lifted the frosted curtain of the space blanket from the same door that last night had been crowded with wolves.

Was that a dream, Hu wondered. His night in the cold had left him groggy and exhausted. He felt as if he had used all the energy his body possessed simply by staying alive through the bitter night.

It had not been a dream. The bodies of the wolves lay covered in the most perfect white snow. Hu allowed himself a satisfied smile.

Then he turned his attention to the songbird.

A man, a soldier obviously, had lifted the rock slab, using a bumper winch on a PLA truck. That was amazing in itself, but Hu had neither the time nor the energy for marvels.

He only knew that the Soviets had found the germs. He watched as the Russian drew his weapon at the mouth of the vault.

Hu's hand stretched out unconsciously for the AK. When he drew it toward him, he realized that he would not be able to kill the man from inside the canopy.

The angles were all wrong.

He couldn't put the muzzle of the AK through either side of the doorjamb and still have enough room to lever the stock and the barrel around to sight on his target.

It didn't matter, anyway.

The Russian had entered the cave.

Hu waited. Despite the fact that he was unseen, his head hunched downward, and his eyes darted from side to side.

Was there only one of them?

Incredibly, it seemed to be true.

Hu popped open the canopy door and stepped into the snow. As soon as he had only his feet to support him, he fell.

They were frozen now. Hu felt the fear wash over him like a cold wave. He knew he would lose his feet.

No matter, he decided.

He dragged himself through the snow, keeping a tight grip on the AK. He would not now be able to follow the Russian into the cave. But, he decided, he would kill the first thing that came out of it.

Hu hunched behind the carcass of the third, the largest, wolf. He let the wind play around him, blowing the soft powder snow into his face while he remained motionless.

Slowly the winter built up a cover of snow over pilot Hu. He was warmer underneath it. Only his eyes and the muzzle of the AK showed over the back of the frozen wolf.

From the mouth of the cave, Hu was invisible.

"IT WILL BE SOON NOW."

Vesh heard Strakhov's voice behind him but had no idea what the Russian was talking about. They had not exactly been keeping up a steady stream of conversation since they'd entered the caves.

Vesh had led off confidently. Strakhov had set a miner's hat at a deliberately uncomfortable angle on his prisoner's head.

Then he had grabbed the sailor's chin in a gloved hand. "Find me the germs," he told Vesh, "or die."

"Don't bullshit me, general," Vesh spat out. "I know I die, anyway."

Strakhov said nothing. He simply pushed the man in front of him, and they descended into the cave.

"I need my hands free," Vesh told him.

"No."

"We will have to climb…"

"No."

They walked down the largest of the Kai-bin galleries toward the ravine. From the map he had seen in Strakhov's quarters, Vesh estimated that they were somewhere far beneath the Harbin airfield.

Vesh was good at maps. He had passed his navigator's exams when he was only fourteen. Only lack of money for the correct bribes had kept his parents from putting Vesh into pilots' school.

Now he put his skill to good use and brought them to the ravine.

"I thought so," Strakhov said behind him.

At first Vesh did not understand, but when he examined the darkness more closely he could see lights. Small lights across the great ravine. Two in front bobbing and weaving as they picked their way down a difficult, winding course.

These would be miners' helmets, Vesh thought. The lights in front moved like the Yugoslav's own light, expressing each jerking movement of the walker's body.

The lights behind were different.

Torches, Vesh decided.

They were brighter and occasionally appeared to lick and pop in bright bursts of flame. Makeshift, Vesh decided.

They were also held in upraised hands.

Although he couldn't see the men who were carrying them, he could tell that the torches were hand held. An extended arm will adjust itself as the walker crosses an uneven terrain. The torches did bob a little but always came back to the same height.

If you had a rifle, Vesh thought, you could kill the men who held the torches by aiming two feet to the left and six inches down. There were four torches.

With a rifle you could get at least half the men.

But Vesh did not want to kill these men. The man he really wanted to kill was right behind him as they reached the Grand Shu ravine.

Behind him, Strakhov saw the edge of the lights and repeated, "I thought so." He brushed Vesh aside and walked farther along the edge of the great trench. His own light jerked violently as he hurried to a good vantage point.

"How many are there?" Strakhov demanded of Vesh. He did not turn. Instead he was counting the bobbing figures whose lights disappeared around corners and then reappeared.

Vesh, kneeling on the ground behind him, strained with his handcuffed hands toward his boot and cursed the appetite that had made him so fat, so inflexible.

He took a deep breath and spoke, trying not to make it sound like a grunt.

"I think there are five," he said helpfully.

"No. There are more than five." Strakhov began counting again.

"Six, then," Vesh said. His fingers were inside the top of his boot. It was difficult to reach between his legs this way, to arch his back for the maximum amount of stretch and grab inside the laced leather for the butt of the palm gun. "Six," he repeated. "Six at the most."

"I've already counted seven," Strakhov snapped impatiently.

Vesh was certain the general was about to turn back toward him. His fingers found the butt and grabbed it. For a moment he touched the trigger and jerked his finger back lest the gun go off in his boot.

But Strakhov did not turn. And the gun did not go off. Vesh now held it in the palm of his right hand. He pulled his fingers from his boot and lurched to his feet with a rocking motion. The weight of his torso brought him off his knees and snapped him back onto his heels.

It was a curiously graceful gesture for an overstuffed man. With the gun carefully concealed in his palm, Vesh felt his confidence had obviously grown.

"Five. Six. Seven. Who gives a shit?" Vesh told Strakhov. "We've got a long trip in front of us. Let's get it done."

Something in the man's voice made the Soviet turn and examine his features. He searched Vesh's face for a sign.

"I don't like you, Russian," Vesh told him. "Your company is obscene."

Strakhov smiled. He had heard this kind of thing before. "You will not have to endure it much longer," he told his prisoner and pushed the man ahead of him.

KNEELING, MUN FELT THE RUSSIAN crouch before her. The Tokarev still pointed at her temple, but it was carelessly held.

He is not Strakhov, Mun thought.

She had read Strakhov's file. She knew the Soviet general was a much different-looking man, a much different man. Inwardly she was sneering at Sergei Strassko.

Why does he tell me he's Strakhov, Mun wondered. She watched the man's eyes, snake eyes, as he kneeled in front of her. She could feel his left hand brush back the fabric of her coat and pinch her nipple between his fingers until it hurt.

He wants to hurt me, Mun thought. He wants to feel powerful and dominant and see me hurt. That is why he uses Strakhov's name. He is weak. He calls himself Strakhov because he fears Strakhov.

He fears Strakhov and wants to be Strakhov.

Mun looked into Strassko's eyes now, not with disgust but with pity. She had changed a great deal since being shut in the tunnel. She saw into this man the way a child sees through the open glass of an ant farm.

Strassko felt the change in her attitude toward him and began to feel uncomfortable. She could not pity him. It was impossible that she could pity him.

He struck her again with the Tokarev. This time Mun let out a sound, a small cry that was less pain than anguish.

Whatever else she knew, she knew she would not let this demon hurt her. She would protect herself. She would breathe her own air.

Strassko grinned at her when she cried out. He gritted his teeth and reached for her with both hands.

Mun felt beside her, near the fire, as Strassko pulled her toward him. She was resisting him, struggling against his domination. She found a stick with her right hand as he was forcing her onto her hurt side. The pain returned.

The end of the stick was hot. It burned the back of her hand even as she swung it. She felt it connect. It caught Strassko full on the left side of the face. He screamed and fell onto his right, lifting the Tokarev from his elbow and leveling it at Mun's pretty face.

She struck him again. Hit him across the forearm with the burning stick and left it on him to burn his arm. Then she stood over him, still clutching the stick. She hit him across the head with it and smelled the fire catch at his hair.

Mun swung the torch underhand and caught the Soviet in the chin. She thought that she would have to kill him, but behind her she felt a gust of air from the cave entrance.

It was open. Escape was possible. She did not have to kill. Not even this.

Despite the pain in her side, Mun flung the torch full into Strassko's face as he felt blindly beside him for the gun. His screams filled the cave now.

Mun could no longer hear her own sobs. She fled, running sideways, running backward, unable to take her eyes off the creature behind her, terrified that Strassko would somehow rise and destroy her even in her escape.

Mun ran up the slope before the vault, under the long shadow of the perpendicular slab of rock.

In front of her, completely invisible in his covering of snow, Hu heard the noise of something exiting the vault.

He switched the AK to automatic fire....

FROM HERE ON, it was easy at least to fool the general. Vesh had never had any idea where the germs were, but now he simply followed the lights of the others as they filed down the ravine.

At last the ledge narrowed so that only a foot of ground was between him and a horrible death.

Vesh stopped and Strakhov bumped into him. The general quickly backed off, but the canny sailor stored that trick. He'd missed the opportunity but it wouldn't happen twice.

"The ledge is too narrow for feet only," Vesh told the general. "I need my hands. Free my hands."

"No." Strakhov was adamant.

"If you don't free my hands, I won't lead you any-more." Vesh said. It was his one bargaining chip. It was a good chip.

Strakhov wouldn't buy it.

"Listen, fool," he snarled. "Walk! Walk now! If you don't walk, I dump you over the side and follow everyone else." Strakhov glanced with disgust toward the small string of lights far across the ravine below them.

Vesh's expression changed. He had not really consid-ered this possibility. It put a whole new slant on things.

Vesh nodded to the general and began to move out. The general followed close behind. Vesh stopped suddenly, and Strakhov once more bumped into him.

This time Strakhov came away wounded.

Vesh pressed the palm gun into the Soviet's abdomen and stepped backward into the man, forcing him down as the trigger was pulled.

Strakhov fell, wounded in the gut. Vesh laughed.

Suddenly the silence of the cave's false night erupted, throwing tracers and muzzle-flashes into the cold belly of darkness.

Vesh ducked immediately. He shucked his helmet and crushed the lens with his foot. Strakhov's was there be-side it. He lifted his foot to crush that one, too, but he heard a voice.

"Goodbye, little fish."

It was Strakhov!

He had a gun!

The madness around them was completely tuned out now. Vesh concentrated only on one thing—his own death, coming down the slope at him from the barrel of Strak-hov's gun.

Ahead, the PLA soldiers were unaware of the conflict happening behind them. They had eyes only for the lights on the helmets of the Executioner and Shu.

Ahead, Strassko lay wounded in the sealed gallery of Kanamuto's ice vault.

Vesh was aware of none of this. He was aware only that he had lost. The pig Russian would win it all. He would come up behind whoever was in front of them and kill them and steal the germs.

And Vesh would die!

"Goodbye, little fish," Strakhov repeated. Vesh brought the heel of his boot down on the lamp and dived sideways into darkness.

There was only a foot of ledge, he knew. The chances of his landing on anything solid were next to nothing, but he had no choice.

He saw Strakhov's muzzle-flash and felt the bullet burn into his shoulder. He saw a second flash and realized he was going to land on the money, on the strip of earth that would preserve him for at least a few more precious seconds.

He landed.

On his shoulder.

The pain passed through him in a terrible wave of nausea, but he fought it back. On the thin strip of ground almost at Strakhov's feet, Vesh cursed his handcuffs and lurched to an upright position.

The palm gun was long gone, but he was a soccer player. He kicked out in the dark and found something human. It moaned. Vesh kicked it again and heard the clatter of metal against rock.

He had lost his gun!

Vesh kicked again and again. He kicked until he was satisfied that he could kick no more. The form on the ground before him exhibited no movement.

Vesh kicked it again to see if it would groan.

It didn't.

Ha! I killed you, you prick, Vesh thought. It was a great relief. He was free now.

He sat on the ground and watched the lights coming back down the opposite slope of the ravine, far ahead of his own position.

Suddenly Vesh Slovincik knew he was not so free.

He was wounded and handcuffed and in the dark.

The only way he could go *anywhere* was by following those lights. He had no idea where those lights were going. He didn't even know whose they were.

All he knew was that the ones behind didn't like the ones in front and the ones behind were armed.

What the hell, the Yugoslav decided, struggling to his feet. Maybe I'll get lucky.

He felt his way along the rock face of the ledge, descending gingerly.

For this first time it occurred to him that he didn't really know what all this was about.

Vesh had gone a distance in the dark when Strakhov moaned and came awake.

By that time the sailor was ninety meters down the slope and couldn't hear it. He never would have found the man, anyway. Except for the flickering lights before him, there was nothing in the blackness. Vesh felt toward the edge of the ridge with his toe. Found it and edged toward it.

At first, there was nothing. His eyes felt as though they were throbbing as they probed the limitless dark.

Then he made out a small butterfly of light, whirling and spinning over and over deep in the darkness of the mine.

Vesh had no idea how deep this great ravine could be, but the length of the fall of that tiny light flickering on and off as it tumbled was dizzying.

He leaned back against the wall, feeling for the reassuring surface of the rock with handcuffed palms. Vesh Slovincik took a deep breath and stilled the fear inside him.

Then he came off the wall and once more felt his way toward the string of lights that would lead him to freedom.

STRASSKO WAS IN AGONY and his clothes were on fire.

He had seen the woman, the Chinese bitch—he had seen her run from the cave. He had struggled to find his pistol to kill her but it was far too late. He was on fire.

His eyes were burning. He howled in the cave and rolled on the cold ground to put out the flames in his clothes.

The fire was *inside* his open coat. He rolled onto his chest and hugged the flame to him, gasping in pain until he could feel the cold of the ground through his smoldering clothes.

Where was his pistol?

Strassko cast his good eye around the floor in the sparse light from the fire. That was it. He had it. The Tokarev was in his hand and he whirled, glancing sideways at the opening to the vault.

Strassko gasped.

The vault was closing.

He scrambled to his feet, hurt and desperate, trying to make the long run down the gallery to the opening before the rock lowered and shut him in forever.

It was too late. He was sealed inside.

Strassko tried to still his fears. He knew someone would have to return for the germs. It was obvious. There were too many people looking for the damn things for him to be sealed in here forever.

Meanwhile he was hurt.

The ache in his head and face and hands was intensified by the worry that the Chinese bitch had blinded him. Damn her.

"Damn her!" Strassko shouted it at the walls and fell immediately silent. He had not liked the amount of fear he heard in his own voice. The pain in his eye shot to the center of his head.

Strassko returned to the place by the fire. He kicked Mun's torch high into the air and kicked at the fire, too.

Then he sat down gingerly, fondling the Tokarev. It was all right, he told himself in a voice that might have passed for calm.

It *is* all right, Strassko thought. I will live. I will get out of this hole alive. I will own these germs *and*, he decided, I will find that bitch and kill her.

Now that he knew what he had to do, he felt better....

From far away he heard noises, stuttering noises, snapping, popping noises and the echo of ricochets like automatic fire.

Automatic fire? Where would it come from?

Strassko looked up the mound of rubble. The torch he had been burned with, the same torch he had kicked in anger, had landed near the roof of Kanamuto's vault at the top of the pile of rubble.

The flame burned bright and leaned all in one direction, the way the flame in a fireplace directs itself toward the flue.

Strassko smiled then.

He knew he would kill that woman yet.

BOLAN LEANED AGAINST THE WALL of the ravine. He had come a long way, but at last they were there.

"It is the extreme right cave," Shu said. "Beneath us is another network of caves, all full of natural gas." Bolan heard the hiss and rasp in the man's voice. He knew Shu had very little time left.

Bolan looked back up the ravine slope. Less than half an hour away on the trail, four lights flickered. He knew the soldiers were closing in, and he knew he had to work fast.

"There is a ledge," Shu told him. "Twenty meters below us. It is very close to the gas. It is well hidden. Climb down to it and set your timer."

Bolan nodded. He was about to speak, but Shu cut him off.

"The way back is over there." The man in his arms gestured to the right. "Set me down here. If you give me your gun—" Shu grinned "—I can make some trouble for them and buy you some time."

"I may need it," Bolan said. "Anyway, it's not over yet."

It was not nearly over.

He let the old man rest against the face of the rock. Shu turned his helmet against the wall so that its light was sheltered, fainter.

Bolan straightened and for a moment missed the weight of carrying the wounded man. But Shu weighed nothing, Bolan thought. And now that he had set him down, Bolan knew the old geologist would not get up again.

He had heard the rattle in the man's voice as he spoke. Five or ten more minutes, Bolan thought.

Shu must have read the Executioner's mind. "It doesn't matter, Comrade Bo-lan. It is the least important thing in the world."

"I hear that," Bolan said.

Behind him there was a rattle of gravel against stone. The Executioner dodged sideways and killed his helmet light. Voices speaking Chinese filled the darkness. Angry, suspicious voices.

Shu's patient voice answered them.

Again the voices snapped into the darkness.

Again Shu's patient tones reached them.

"What are they saying?" Bolan asked. He moved as he spoke, and it was good that he moved. Tracers from a Chinese Type 47 chewed at the rock where he'd crouched.

Again Bolan talked to the night. He shouted at Shu, unsure how to judge the range of his voice in the hollow darkness.

"Tell them," Bolan shouted. The tracers once again chewed up the ground near him.

"Tell them I have a thermonuclear device." The thwup-thwup-wang of automatic fire respected nothing. It was mindless.

"Tell them!" Bolan said, his voice suddenly shaking with rage. *"They put down their popguns, or I cook us all."*

The Chinese could understand no English but the message carried. In the silence of the big caves, Bolan's voice was echoed over and over.

The only other sound was the sound of Shu laughing.

13

Hu steadied his aim over the frozen carcass of the big wolf. He let his tired brain shut down its nervousness and simply lived for the moment when a head would appear over the snow-covered stone and he would shoot it.

A lot of things had occurred to him when he had first heard the Russian voice. At first he thought that acting now was too much. It was more than could be expected of him. It was inhuman that he should have to torture himself by moving this way and leaving the soft, velvet glove of cold-induced sleep.

Then he had come awake.

There were two reasons he had to kill now, Hu knew. One was simply because there was no one else to do the job and the job had to be done.

The Soviets must not get the germs.

The second reason was also very simple. Hu needed to focus on something to stay awake and alive. He needed a task to rise to or the sleep would take him.

Hu knew how tempting sleep was. It was a sleep like opium to an addict. It was a sleep like being warm forever inside a black velvet glove.

Hu also knew it was a sleep from which he would never return.

He heard the noises of someone exiting the cave. He let his mind assess the noises, let his feeling, not his intellect, tell him the precise moment when the Soviet's head would appear over the lip of the cave.

A head appeared.

The barrel of the AK was directly aligned with the emerging head as Hu squeezed the trigger.

It was the woman.

Miraculously nothing happened. Hu stared at the gun in his hands, wondering what had gone wrong. If he had been more alert he would have recognized the problem by its sound but in truth he had never heard that sound before.

The AK had jammed.

Mun left the cave, looking backward. She did not see him. She was staring back into the cave with a look of stark terror on her face.

The Russian must be following her.

Hu tried to speak, to shout to her but he found his voice had dried up sometime during the night.

He swallowed and lapped some snow off the dead wolf's back. "The winch!" he croaked. "Let it go!"

Mun started toward him, but Hu brought the weapon up and threatened her. "The winch, idiot!"

She turned and ran up the slope to the truck while Hu tried to unjam the Kalishnikov with frozen fingers. What a pleasant change it was, he thought, for that woman to listen to someone else.

What a nice surprise.

The rock slab lowered before Strassko could exit.

Now Mun was running back down the slope toward him, saying, "Captain X. Oh, Captain X..."

"I am Hu," he croaked. His words didn't seem to affect her. She was holding him, kissing him. It was nice, he thought, but it was not the time.

"Go to the truck." But Mun was not listening. She was simply holding him, holding him and rocking back and forth, crouched on the frozen body of the great wolf.

Hu slapped her leg.

Mun looked at him with fire in her eyes. Hu saw the hatred rise in her face and he smiled.

It felt like the first smile after a long winter of bitterness.

"Later," Hu said.

Mun smiled, too.

"Now," Hu told her, "go to the truck. Radio your father. Tell him we have found the germs. Then," he added, "start the truck. You must turn on the heater, too. The switch is on the right side of the wheel, next to the choke.

"Turn it on high," Hu told her. "As high as it will go. Then come back and get me. You will have to drag me with the winch to the truck."

Mun's face looked puzzled.

"Just do it. Please," Hu asked.

Mun Giyang nodded and raced up the slope to the truck.

Hu had no idea what had happened inside the cave but it did not seem bad.

He wondered what it was going to feel like to be dragged by a winch over rocks.

FOR A LONG TIME, Strakhov lay in the darkness, gathering strength. He seemed to be floating, at first. He could feel the pain of his body but that was a distant thing, as distant as the lights so far away in the darkness.

Strakhov followed the lights and felt himself slipping away with them. The air was all cold around him and it was growing colder.

Strakhov could feel a movement in the air. How strange, he thought distractedly. There is no entrance here. He had enough consciousness left to handle such information, but he handled it in a dreamy and detached way.

He had no sense of time. He could not have said how long he lay on the ridge overhanging the great ravine, but he remained there motionless, until he heard a booming voice echoing through the cave below.

Strakhov knew that voice!

He rolled on his side toward the lights and felt *his* presence immediately. It was strong here. Much stronger than it had ever been. Much, much stronger than the mere nagging doubt that had caused the Soviet general to leave Brooklyn.

What was the voice saying? What did it mean, "cook us all?"

Strakhov's scalp suddenly tingled, and he came immediately awake.

He knew exactly what Bolan had meant.

Bolan had the bomb!

It had been such a sensitive issue that Strakhov had trusted no one with full knowledge of it. Molinz! Well, Molinz was a fool. Strakhov had told him nothing.

But Strassko had known a little. Strassko had known it was explosives.

And now Bolan had it! Bolan was going to touch off the fastburn and destroy everything. Greb Strakhov included.

The pain of the Yugoslav's kicks slowed movement to a crawl. But slowly, certainly, Strakhov turned on his side and made his way upward, following the current of the moving air.

He did not know how much time there was.

He only knew that Mack Bolan, the man he had come to know as the Executioner, the only man Greb Strakhov genuinely regretted encountering...*that* man, Strakhov knew, *would* blow up the caves.

Even if he himself was in them!

Strakhov was crawling uphill now. Very fast.

LING AND HAN WERE INSIDE THE TRANSPORT when the call came in.

The control tower was patching through all communication to the cockpit. Ling recognized Mun's voice immediately. He remembered he had not seen her since that day in his office.

Had it been yesterday or the day before?

Now he heard her emotional voice over the radio. He knew something was wrong. He had never heard her cry since her mother had died.

"Stop it!" he snapped. "There is no time. Give me the facts." He was sorry to do it. He hated shaming her that way. But it was necessary.

"Sorry, Father," Mun said.

Ling caught something very new in her voice and sat forward attentively. His brow furrowed as Mun's story unfolded.

They had the germs. Yes.

There was a wounded pilot and a Soviet agent and so much more that nothing made sense.

When Mun went off the air, Ling ordered Han to remain guarding the transport. Then he went back to the radio and ordered arms and men to the Imperial Testing Facility. And, oh yes, a Medivac.

Ling left Han in the cockpit and moved back through the transport toward the hydraulic ramp.

He paused momentarily beside the empty open crate. Intelligence specialists had already been all over that crate. Ling knew *exactly* what it had carried.

Atomics!

It was a highly specialized type of bomb. It was well-known the superpowers had such things. The Americans called them SADM—Special Atomic Demolition Munitions. They were expressly intended for behind-the-lines activities during a ground assault in Europe.

The United States had at least two hundred such devices.

Ling had no idea how many the Soviets had, or what they called them. It didn't matter. Nobody used the American word SADM, anyway.

They were just called "backpack bombs."

And the Soviets dared to use them here.

The ramp was down now. Ling shot a backward glance of pure hatred at the crate. Then he was gone. A helicopter would take him to his daughter.

VESH WATCHED THE FOUR TORCHES move in unison toward the threatening voice.

He had no idea what the voice had meant about "cook," but he knew what the tone of it meant and he knew whom it belonged to.

Him again, Vesh thought.

I cannot get rid of him. A surge of hatred broke into his mind. He thought of the complete humiliation of being locked in the trunk with the dead man.

Then the hatred broke and vanished.

Vesh had another memory.

It was the memory of his fear on the night of the storm when he had first met this man with the voice, the man Strakhov called Bolan.

Vesh cringed at the memory of his own cowardice and turned his mind to the gun that Bolan had left in his boot. It was stupid, but he felt as if Bolan had known that he was going to be able to use it.

He had been able to tell, after all, when Vesh was thinking about pulling it on him in the empty hold....

Vesh dismissed these thoughts. They were crazy. He knew he was going a little buggy from feeling his way through the darkness for too long.

He had also lost a lot of blood.

There were four soldiers together now and Bolan was somewhere else, somewhere in shadow, holding some kind of threat over all their heads.

The last of the PLA soliders had come down the slope slowly. They were holding two torches each. It was a good trick, Vesh thought. A good way to trick Bolan.

He had known there were four men all along. He could see their torches.

Two men had run ahead in the darkness to ambush him.

But he had ambushed them.

Now another voice, an old voice, was speaking Chinese in very reasonable tones. Vesh brushed down the rock face past the palaver and edged his way around the circle of men.

He wanted to work his way back up the side that Bolan had come from and he wanted to steal a lamp.

There was one lying on the ground and he approached it. As he passed the last of the tunnels he felt a rush of fresh air come out of the tunnel mouth toward him. There was also noise. A woman faintly yelling...

The others did not hear it because they were nowhere close to him. But Vesh heard it, heard it and moved toward it.

It was a way out.

Also, the woman sounded as if she needed help.

Vesh slipped past the group of soldiers and into the tunnel mouth.

"TELL THEM TO HOLD UP THEIR HANDS," Bolan told Shu. "Tell them to tell the ones behind them, too."

Shu translated, laughing. It was too good to be true, in a way. In all his long life he had never had this much excitement! This man, Bo-lan, certainly did live well.

It seemed good to Shu that he was ending his life on such a high note, with such adventure. He did not mind dying in the caves. They were his life! How many people would have a monument as enormous as the Grand Shu ravine?

He shouted at the soldiers to stand away from their arms. He waited until the others came into range. There were only two, he noticed, but they carried two torches each. Clever, he acknowledged to himself. They would have made good students!

Shu did not notice a dark shadow stealing toward his helmet. Or that, at the last moment, it moved away from the helmet and into the vault cave.

There was too much going on, and the geologist Shu wanted to take it all in before he died.

"Arm the bomb," he told Bolan. "Do it while I'm alive. I want to know."

He could not see the American. He was hiding in the shadows. But Shu did hear the big man's voice.

"I'll see ya in the next life, *droog* Shu!"

"Decidedly." Shu answered. "*Bredovnia* Bo-lan."

Shu could hear nothing more from his companion, but he knew the man was free-climbing the twenty meters down the rock face toward the ledge where he would arm the bomb.

He was almost ready to die.

In the darkness Vesh felt something brush past him and it stank. It smells like burned flesh, he thought.

There was a shrill yelp of fright when the thing touched him, but it kept going.

It could have been human, Vesh thought. He listened to the receding figure. The noises were the noises of footsteps....

Vesh continued blundering through the dark. There was still an air current, but it had dwindled remarkably. He was considering retracing his steps. He was wondering if he had lost his way completely and would now die in the Harbin ice caves.

That was something else that had been bothering him, Vesh decided. Why had Strakhov called these the ice caves? Up until now he had seen very little ice....

Vesh stopped walking and concentrated on making no sound. He could no longer hear the distressed woman's voice that twenty minutes ago had led him down this course.

There was nothing now. Nothing except the diminished air current, the footsteps of the thing that he had brushed into, the sound of his own ragged breath and the knowledge that this cave sloped downward.

Vesh continued down the slope. At least, he decided, he knew what he had come from. There was no way out there.

Perhaps this way led out.

He was holding on to this hope dearly when he encountered a turn in the cave wall. He knew it was a turn because there was a slight light flickering high above his head on the cave ceiling.

Hope kindled with that light.

Vesh started to run.

He rounded the corner and confronted the steep slope of the rubble wall. His hope failed.

Handcuffed as he was, Vesh knew he would never be able to climb that mound of stones alone.

The hard wall of stone was the face of death. Vesh touched his tombstone in the darkness.

He was dispirited. He felt he had shot his wad and come up with nothing. It was all right, he decided. He had known it could end this way. The truth was, he told himself, he had never really expected otherwise.

Vesh Slovincik knelt on the floor. He knew that if he sat back on his hams, he'd never be able to get up again. It's a hard enough thing for a fit man to do. For a man who carries extra weight, it was nearly impossible.

At least, Vesh thought, I am allowed to have a light. He looked at the ceiling and took a great deal of comfort from the flickering fire inside the sealed vault.

He was bone tired. The walk and the struggle and the cold and his confinement had all taken their toll. Vesh's head slumped forward onto his chest. To anyone looking at him from above it must have seemed that Vesh Slovincik was praying.

He remembered the last time he had prayed. It had been the night of the storm aboard the *Tito I*. Death had been so close to him then that the death represented by the rock wall seemed less threatening somehow.

The night Bolan had saved him from the wave; Vesh Slovincik had faced a truly big death, the whole of the Pacific Ocean had moved to swallow him up, and he had been saved only by the most absurd chance.

Behind him, Vesh heard the faint echo of two shots, a sput-sput noise that rolled like a pinball off the surface of the walls.

Vesh had no idea what the shots meant. He had no idea what he was hoping for or what he was going to do. He wasn't thinking. He was beyond that.

Vesh Slovincik got to his feet and began to move.

He left the comfort of the faint light and once again moved up the slope, in the direction of the gunfire, toward the American called Bolan.

14

Bolan felt his way down through the dark. The deeper he went the more he was reminded of Vietnam, of the nights in the jungle when death sat in his lap and whispered in his ear. He knew the feeling of darkness pulling at the mind, when all there was to call his own was fear and loneliness.

Bolan had a backpack so destructive it felt like death itself clinging to him. For some reason, it felt familiar. Even since the hellish experience of the circus in Nam, Bolan had felt that monkey holding tight. He, of all people, knew how fragile life is, how death waits to snatch away the soul in an unguarded moment. That was the central insight that formed Mack Bolan's insides—the sadness, and the hardness. So different were these qualities, and yet they were inseparable.

To Bolan, fate was playing a cruel joke, but the Executioner was twisting that joke around until it came out his way.

Bolan hated the germs and all they represented. If he had to go with them in the moment of reckoning, he would. He had never expected otherwise.

Bolan went deeper into the darkness and took the backpack with him.

He could not see much as he descended the rock face.

The air was colder here, much colder than it had been on the ledge above. He still wore the miner's helmet. The wide

aluminum brim clinked constantly on the rock face in front
of him.

It was a stupid design for this kind of work, the Executioner decided. It resembled a World War I infantry helmet. In tight spaces like this one, in which his face was
pressed against the rock, the brim just made maneuvering
awkward.

Still, Bolan was grateful for the light. He was having
enough difficulty finding toeholds and handholds and
balancing the weight of the bomb on his back without
trying to move in complete darkness.

His left foot touched something flat and solid, and he
moved backward, hoping at last he had come to Shu's
ledge.

He had.

He brought his right foot down and released his grip on
the rock face. The climb back would be easier without the
weight, without *both* weights, Bolan decided. The second
weight he was thinking of was the weight of the mission.

As soon as he armed the bomb, he had accomplished
what he had set out to do. Afterward he would concern
himself with his own safety, or with killing Strakhov, or
whatever.

It felt good to have the job done.

Bolan turned his face from the rock wall, and the light
on his helmet caught a shimmer on the walls of the ravine
far below him.

He moved the two meters to the edge of the ledge and
shucked the rucksack while he examined the ravine from
this new vantage point.

It was wonderful.

An enormous crystalline glacier, one as large as any

Bolan had ever seen, and with the diamond-clear surface of highly burnished ice rested at eye level about half a kilometer away.

The edge of the glacier tipped over the edge of the ravine like a frozen waterfall. Bolan's eyes followed its descent into the depths of the cave, until his weak light would follow it no more.

Bolan had the impression that he had just seen the tip of this glacier. It could be as large as the ravine itself, he thought. It could be what had carved the ravine in the first place.

At last the Executioner understood the word "grand" in Shu's name for this place. He had not known the man well. All along he had simply thought that Shu was being playful.

It was that, Bolan thought. Shu was certainly a lively guy. But it was also the man's sense of beauty, and his eye for a beauty that no one else could see.

The Executioner was impressed.

He was impressed, too, by the knowledge that his bomb would change this place forever. Shu would have known that as well, Bolan thought.

The aged geologist had been willing to give this up all along to destroy the germs.

Bolan's thoughts were broken by the sound of shots above him. He had no idea what this new development was. It sounded like trouble, but that was nothing new.

He would face the trouble later. Right now he had to finish the job.

Bolan leaned over the backpack and his headlamp caught the insignia of whirling atoms that had so alarmed those first Chinese guards at the Harbin airfield.

The airfield seemed a world away now.

Bolan stripped back the nylon slicker that covered the device. Its detonator was a conventional fail-safe one.

Once armed, it could not be disarmed.

Bolan allowed himself five hours and set the liquid crystal clock. The red digital numbers blipped on and off. Despite their faintness, the color of them hurt Bolan's eyes.

It was as if the numbers themselves were radioactive.

Bolan took a moment to recheck his calculations. Barring anything unexpected, he knew it would take him five hours maximum to clear out of this cave.

He primed the bomb. The clock began counting. Bolan stood and moved to the rock face, thinking of Shu twenty meters above him.

Bolan hoped that the caves would absorb the explosion so that there would be no poisonous fallout.

He was glad the old man had not told him the secret of this place before he experienced it. He had a special grace, that old man.

Bolan realized he had been thinking of the man in the past tense. He knew then that Shu was dead.

THIS TUNNEL WAS WARMER, much warmer. But there was a price....

Strakhov dragged himself up the pathway. The air current blew on his face but his blood-caked hair remained immobile.

The space he was crawling through was narrow and was filled with guano, bat droppings, the price he had to pay for the warmer air. Strakhov could hear the bats screech around him as he pulled himself up the slope.

He had let out a cry of terror as the first two or three of them had fluttered against his face.

Now that he knew what they were, he was not terrified. He was disgusted. Strakhov did not know which was worse.

The first two or three bats in his face had shocked and weakened him. Their flight had set off the flight of the entire population of the cave.

Hundreds of bats had swirled and crowded past Strakhov's supine form, dropping their guano and beating their wings on him as they passed in the narrow space.

It seemed like the madness had gone on for hours. Now all that was left was Strakhov and the long line of bat shit that led to the surface and the little creatures' escape.

Strakhov was weak, wounded and covered in shit.

He was also madder than hell.

It was a good thing he was madder than hell.

It gave him fight and fire. Strakhov dragged his broken form up the slope, and ahead of him he could now see *bright* light. An opening, he decided. Freedom!

Strakhov went at the remaining few meters with a renewed will.

He had his head out of the cave now. And his shoulders. Strakhov twisted around, getting a fix on his location.

He was in a sinkhole. A sinkhole near the airport! Across the field he could see a Soviet transport waiting waiting for him! The ramp in its belly was wide open. All he had to do was get there.

The pain in his abdomen doubled him over as he tried to kick free of the cave.

Strakhov knew he had lost a lot of blood. He also knew he would survive.

If it is only a matter of strength and will, Strakhov decided, *I will survive*. He pulled himself free of the cave and lay gasping on the ground.

He heard boots crunch in the snow beside him and whirled suddenly.

The man was a PLA solider on patrol. The same man who yesterday had tried to close the airport gate on Bolan.

Strakhov moaned and collapsed.

The man behind him saw the blood on the snow beside the Russian. He could also see Strakhov was unarmed.

With something like compassion he moved closer to the wounded man. He crouched beside the general and made the mistake of reaching out, of touching him, trying to turn him over...

SHU WAS DYING. On the ground before him lay the four PLA soldiers. Shu had already ordered them to disarm. Now all he had to do was wait for Comrade Bolan's return.

Then everything could be left to him.

He was a good man, this Bo-lan, Shu decided.

He wondered if the man's spirit could be moved by the secret of Shu's ravine.

Suddenly there was a movement at his right hand. A figure burst from the germ cave entrance into the gloom.

Shu was not sure whether it was human. It seemed to be in great pain.

Then he saw the gun. It was human.

"Freeze," said Strassko. His white breath spilled into the lighted air between them.

Shu laughed. There was something absurd about this man telling him to freeze in an ice cave.

But Strassko wasted no more time. He snapped off two shots that ended Shu's life. One of the PLA soldiers turned back toward him, and Strassko shot him, too.

He was in a bloody frenzy. He could smell and taste warm blood in this cold, dark cave. Strassko was on the kill.

He did not waste time with the soldiers. Eventually they could lead him out of the cave. He had enough of the vials in his coat pockets to still make this little enterprise pay.

There was a noise over the edge of the ravine. Strassko backed toward it, covering the soldiers with the Tokarev.

A light was coming up the ravine wall toward him. A helmet light.

Strassko decided to wait for the climber to appear. Maybe he would know a way out. Maybe he would know something, anything, that Strassko could turn to his advantage.

The game in China was getting very close. Strassko decided he needed a lucky number....

HU WAS JUST BEGINNING TO FEEL THE PAIN when Ling arrived with his men.

His tissues, which had been extensively frozen during the night, had not caused him any pain until now. Why should they, he thought. They were as good as dead.

Now, however, with the heat from the vents in the truck, Hu was coming to know the incredible pain of frostbite. His left arm ached, too, where the first wolf had bitten him.

His eyes teared with pain. Hu knew from the events of last night that he was not weak. Still he cried. The pain was too great.

There were some consolations.

Mun was there. She was soft and warm and she smelled good. Also, Hu noticed, she had very little on underneath her coat. That would bear further investigation when he felt better.

There was some fruit, too. The Russian had provided him with the first meal he'd eaten in more than a day, and he was grateful.

When Ling arrived he found his daughter holding a frozen man in her arms with the tenderness he had sometimes known in her mother.

Strange events, Ling decided. Despite his daughter's beauty, he knew she was not popular with men. He knew the reason, too. His daughter was a bitch. He could think that and still love her.

Mun explained more of the situation after Ling had joined them in the cab. The germs were inside the vault. He knew that now. He also knew that he could destroy them himself with the Soviet bomb if he could get his hands on it.

Strakhov had dealt him a winning card! Once the general brought atomic weapons into the picture, Ling could do what he wanted and simply blame it on the Russians. Nobody, not even the secretary, would doubt him.

Ling ordered the men to winch the rock slab away again. They started loading the crates very carefully onto the truck.

Ling was going to hold the power now.

STRAKHOV LEFT THE DEAD GUARD where he lay and wiped the gore from the middle finger of his right hand.

It was the simplest maneuver. It required no strength, only timing and knowledge, which was good because Strakhov's strength was almost played out.

Whatever he was running on now, it was not a physical force. Strakhov himself knew that. He had felt this way before. In Leningrad as a young man, he had felt this way. The troops had fought for days and weeks on end without sleep or food.

In the end they fought without bullets. They just fought. Now Strakhov fought like that again.

He dragged the guard's AK toward him and struggled to his feet. He rubbed a handful of snow onto the wound and felt the sting replaced by numbness.

He did it again.

Then, leaning on the AK, Strakhov made his way toward the transport....

BOLAN'S HEAD CLEARED THE LEDGE and suddenly his left eye was looking straight into the barrel of a pistol—a Soviet weapon, he decided. Czech. An old Tokarev.

Bolan looked past the gun to the man.

At first, he did not recognize Strassko. The man's flesh and hair and clothes were burned. Even the hand holding the gun was burned.

But there was something about the eyes. Something hard and something crazy. Bolan knew him from the *Tito I*. It was the coward who had raped Reiko. Bolan smelled Strassko's fetid breath and the burned clothes.

Bolan brushed past the gun and raised himself onto the ledge until he was crouched in front of the man.

"What were you doing there?" Strassko demanded. He jerked the pistol nervously toward the edge.

"I was arming the bomb, Strassko," Bolan said.

Now the man recognized him. The Executioner had been clean shaven in Montreal, but the time at sea and the events of these past few days had changed that. The man looked older with a beard, less handsome maybe, but more Russian, more trustworthy.

"What bomb?" Strassko asked the man before him. He did not like the way Bolan was crouching. The man seemed to be poised for action. His hands were splayed beside him like a high diver in a crouch before he executed a perfect dive.

"Don't move!" Strassko warned him nervously. "What bomb?" he again demanded.

"Strakhov put a nuclear device on your transport. I stole it."

"Fastburn!" Strassko said.

"Fastburn," Bolan agreed.

Strassko laughed. "But it will never work, American. The tunnel is blocked!" He laughed viciously, and Bolan bridled at the laughter. The Executioner might have played his hand then, but Strassko was much too smart for that.

"It is a backpack bomb?" Strassko asked him.

"Uh-huh."

"Disarm it."

"Can't be done," Bolan told the man above him. "They take one set of numbers and that's all."

"Do you know the way out?" Strassko yelled desperately.

Bolan smiled.

Behind the Russian's back there was a noise. Bolan looked up over the man's shoulder.

"It won't work," Strassko said disgustedly.

The noise happened again. This time it was closer.

Strassko turned slightly and the Executioner swung, using his arms as clubs. Strassko caught the motion in time and tried to back off from it but he was hit, butted from behind.

Someone pushed into him and forced him into the full impact of the American's kick. His chin snapped skyward. He could feel the disastrous crack in his neck.

The force of the kick sent both men backward onto the ground.

"Get him off me!" Vesh Slovincik shouted at the American. "Get him off, you bastard!"

Bolan had rolled free of his kick, but he was still on the ground. He came to his knees quickly and faced the inert form of Strassko draped across the second man. He looked more closely.

It was the sailor from the *Tito I*.

The man who had once tried to kill him after he had been rescued was the same man who had now helped him.

It didn't seem to make much sense.

"Bastard American prick face!" Vesh was shouting. "Get him off."

Bolan had to laugh. He held the torso of the dying Russian as Vesh Slovincik rolled free, still cursing.

"Let me live," Strassko asked him.

Bolan grinned. "Sure thing, buddy," he told the man. He set the Russian's head gently on the cold ground and turned to face the sailor.

Vesh was on his knees, eyeing the American suspiciously. "I helped you for a change and you treat me like this!" the man screamed at him. "You don't leave me lying around with any more corpses!" Vesh shouted. "Never again!"

Bolan fumbled inside his jacket for a shirt pocket and pulled out some Marlboros. He lit two and stuck a lighted one between the lips of the handcuffed, kneeling man.

"Thanks," he said. He meant it.

Vesh stopped yelling. "Is okay." He paused. "I owe you, eh?"

"No." Bolan said. "Not anymore."

"Is it true what this one says about the tunnel?" Vesh asked the American. "What do you think, eh? What are we going to do?"

"Do you speak any Chinese?" Bolan asked.

"Fuck your mother," Vesh said. It was good to laugh.

15

Han was trying to raise Ling on the radio. All he got was one of the pilots at the testing facility.

They were trying to lift a stone. There was something about a cave sealed by a stone, but Han couldn't make out much from the pilot's talk.

The man was too excited.

"Look, just get Ling!" he said. But the man continued giving him a blow-by-blow account of the wooden crates being unloaded. Han rolled his eyes disgustedly and turned to stare directly into the cockpit window.

He did not see the man behind him.

Strakhov wrapped the belt from his trousers around Han's neck quickly. The speed of his action was incredible for a wounded man. It was necessary speed. The speed and agility of sheer desperation. Han died.

Strakhov tossed him out of the pilot's seat and rested, holding on to the back of the chair.

He knew he could get back down the plane and close down the noisy ramp. He knew he could make it back to the cockpit and he knew he had enough left to get this four-prop monster into the air and headed to Russia.

After that, it was anybody's game.

Strakhov wheezed on the back of the chair. Suddenly his eyes came level with a small box secured on a shelf above the navigator's table.

Medical supplies. He scrambled for it desperately, with shaking, liver-spotted hands. He caressed the box. It was safety. It was his ticket home.

Inside it, Strakhov found exactly what he was looking for. He unfastened his belt from Han's neck and tied off his elbow, pumping the forearm back and forth until he raised a swollen vein.

The morphine in the disposable syringe hit his system like a blessing from God. The general leaned back, secure.

It was okay. It was okay now. He could kill the pain. He could concentrate a while longer. He could get home.

Greb Strakhov opened his pants at the fly and broke the seal on another 10 cc syringe.

He dug the syringe into the flesh surrounding his wound with the precision of a man who has worked long, hard hours in a field hospital. The pain of the needle as it bit into his skin was good. It was the promise of the sweet relief to come.

Strassko leaned back, sated.

He would move in a moment, but for now he had earned his rest.

THE PLA SOLDIERS WORKED LIKE BEARS under Bolan's gestured guidance. They all worked.

Bolan had shot the handcuffs off Vesh with an AK. Then he had handed the weapons back to the soldiers. They seemed to understand.

The man needed them, needed their trust and their effort if they were to win and come out of this alive.

I wonder if they have any idea what it's all about, Bolan thought.

He imagined they must. They worked hard enough.

Vesh had been able to communicate a little of what was going on to them by constantly tapping his watch and making boom noises. There'd certainly been an improvement in the man.

Bolan was getting to like the sailor.

By chance they had missed Strassko's passage—wide enough for a man to crawl through. Pulling off rubble, they had blocked it and now the rocks in the tunnel seemed endless. At first they'd all simply climbed the mound of rubble and kicked the free stones loose. They'd disturbed the rock around them when they did that.

Plumes of smoke shot down from the cave roof on more than one occasion, but they all knew they couldn't stop. Finally, when they had leveled off the top of the pile, they made a chain of five men and passed the rocks behind them until the tunnel to the rear was half full of rubble. Still there seemed no end to the rock that trapped them.

He looked at his watch. Their time was nearly up.

Then they heard voices, very faintly, and some activity ahead.

Ling stood in the half light, urging the soldiers on. They worked like ants, carrying the crates out in a stream. Under the winched rock and up the hill they carried them: box after box of poison. The truck was filling.

With each vibration of the truck, the frozen pilot in the front seat moaned louder. His feet were thawing out. The pain was shooting up his legs like an electric current.

"Move!" ordered Ling. The excitement was building in him. There was nothing to stop him now.

The troops carried on. Ling pored over the crates as if they contained something precious and magic and not liquid death.

"I want these," he said, pointing to a row marked For Russian Subjects.

The pilot was crying out in pain and Ling deplored the nuisance.

"And I want these," he said of the next row.

It was marked For American Subjects.

BOLAN WORKED WITH RENEWED VIGOR, taking the heaviest rocks himself. With each rock removed, the voices seemed to be nearer.

Or were the voices a hallucination brought on by the desperation and the darkness? The soldiers seemed to hear them, too. The Yugoslav worked as if his life depended on it. Bolan had spent an eternity in the cave.

He was working too fast to check the time.

LING HEARD THE TUMBLING OF ROCKS on the other side of the cave-in. And then their voices.

The troops heard them, too—Chinese voices. They stopped, crates in hand, and listened.

"Hello! Can you hear me?" shouted one.

Ling hissed furiously. They were almost done. And he had too many witnesses already.

"Keep working. It's a trick," he ordered.

The troops looked at him dubiously. They wanted more than anything to pull the rocks away and save their brothers. One by one they hefted the crates again and went back to work.

Ling held back until he saw the slab lowered across the entrance. It sat heavily, a monument to him.

AT THE SOUND OF AN ENGINE, Bolan and the soldiers redoubled their efforts. A narrow passage was cleared. Ahead they could see faint light—daylight, and the outline of shelving.

"Let me check it out," Bolan said, moving ahead into Kanamuto's chamber for the first time.

He walked past the shelving marked with Japanese writing, which he partially understood. He ignored it all.

Vesh rushed to the big rock. "How much do you figure it weighs?" Bolan asked him.

"In kilos?" Vesh said amazed. "Who knows? We can't lift it, Bolan. Nobody can lift that."

"Maybe not straight up," the Executioner told him. "But why can't we slide it away?"

Vesh nodded appreciatively. *That* had never occurred to him.

Ling stood on the running board of the truck. He was trying to give the driver his orders but the pilot was screaming so loud that the words were garbled in the driver's mind.

"Ben Sho Research Institute. Don't stop, whatever you do."

"Ben Sho? But that is a classified institute. We can't enter there," said the driver.

"I will be there when you arrive. Don't stop, and don't look in the crates," said Ling. "And I want every man to report to me personally."

The driver nodded, moving the truck off in a rumble. Ling dropped off the running board and headed down the hill. The helicopter was warming up. The rotors swept slowly and powerfully.

As Ling came to the rock slab he jumped onto it.

The slab moved.

Ling looked quickly to the pilot. The bird would not be able to lift off for another minute.

The slab moved again.

Ling heard an American shouting and the grunts of men as they heaved.

Ling ran to the copter and pulled out an assault rifle. When he turned around with the AR in his hands he faced two Chinese soldiers. Then a third. They looked back at him in amazement, blinking in the sunlight.

Then a Westerner exited. He smelled bad and his hands were shackled but the shackles had been sheared off.

Another Westerner exited and Ling knew immediately that this was the leader, the one with the voice. Ling looked into the stone eyes of the rugged face and knew that the man had waited to be the last man out.

Ling decided the man had been doing that for much of his life.

"I don't know who you are, fella," Bolan said to the spy chief, who stood with the AK in his hands. "But we'd all better lose this place right away."

"Fastburn?" Ling asked him. They couldn't see the gun. They were all blinded by the white snow and the sun.

"Yeah, that's what Shu called it," Bolan said. "Fastburn."

"And the Soviet bomb?" Ling asked him, troubled. He still did not know whom he was talking to.

Bolan's watch had stopped.

Ling sprang for the chopper as he yelled for the pilot to lift off. He made the cockpit just as it ascended the snow.

IT WAS COLD in the transport plane.

The morphine and the exhaustion were taking their toll.

The plane was on auto-pilot, but it bucked and rocked in the bitter Asian wind.

Strakhov was having trouble controlling it even in his lucid moments. But they were getting further and further apart.

He was close to the Soviet Union now. No. Wait. He checked his charts. He was *over* the Soviet Union.

Strakhov knew he could not control things any longer. He knew that he would have to put it down.

He tried to concentrate, tried to find a good spot out of the cockpit window. But his airspeed was very high for visual recon, and he was still over timber country. Then he saw something—a structure.

It didn't matter. He couldn't keep it together. He was going in....

From deep within his consciousness Strakhov felt the impact. It seemed to go on forever in a slow dream. Then there was quiet, and the blackness.

Somewhere a voice said, "He's alive." The words were Russian. Who was alive?

How long had he been hearing Russian? Strakhov felt the warm hand and the needle as they tried to raise a vein. Who was alive?

BOLAN KNEW. They all knew. The light was too bright to see, but they knew the chopper was lifting off and that it was their only ticket out of the inferno

Two of the soldiers made the cockpit. Bolan and the others could only grasp the landing runners. The chopper's might lifted them straight into the air, pulling at their shoulders.

Vesh jumped for one of the runners but missed and fell in the snow.

Then he felt the rumbling. The earth growled angrily and then gaped. A massive jet of steam and water shot up around him.

The world collapsed with a sickening drop. Then the explosion blasted everything apart.

The chopper was sucked down in the rush of the collapse but it struggled to rise. Bolan looked down between his boots, the image emblazoned on his mind: Vesh scrambled across the collapsing terrain and then was lost in the steam and water. And then, just as it had collapsed in a giant sinkhole miles across, the world seemed to burst apart in a horrendous explosion.

Bolan felt the heat rise.

The chopper was struggling upward. Each man was mesmerized by the awesome, angry hell that exploded up at the tiny bird.

Rock half vaporized with heat came spinning upward. Bolan watched it grow furiously as it came at them.

The pilot panicked and wrenched the stick to the side. Bolan caught a boot in the head as the bird tilted; he felt something give in his shoulder.

The chopper was blown sideways by a pillar of fire that dwarfed anything Bolan had seen in his life.

Then the chopper stopped.

The fire blew upward but sucked in air at the bottom in a cataclysmic hurricane. The chopper was being sucked down in the rush; it trembled and shook as the pilot fought to keep airborne.

They hung there on the edge of death, hardly moving as they fought the fierce wind. The fire painted them in orange and yellow as they hung against the dark sky.

They rose slowly. They had been on the edge.

In the respite, they managed to pull up and wrap their legs around the runners. Now they flew through the chill air with the pillar of fire at their backs.

Bolan's head cleared when his hand slipped. Something was wrong with his shoulder, and in the cold he could not control his hand.

Still they held on, each in his own battle of will against the cold and the thump of the copter. Below the terrain went on endlessly—small trees and snow in the hills. Here and there was a road or a cluster of buildings.

For a while they flew over an army truck that inched along far below. The soldiers were trying to figure out which unit the truck was with and where it was headed. There was no consensus. No one really wanted to talk in the chill wind.

The copter dipped, flew closer to the truck and then banked away. Bolan reconned. Ahead was a large square institution. He still had not figured out one thing that troubled him.

Why were there so many footsteps at the mouth of the cave?

16

The man in the space suit passed the scanner over Bolan and then did the same with each of the soldiers. They were in the basement of the complex and still did not know where they were or when they would get out. Two of the soldiers were sobbing—the fear of radiation poisoning was somehow more frightening than a firefight. Bolan was impatient.

Ling passed in the control room beyond the glass, and Bolan shouted to him. Ling answered over the intercom.

"Can you get me radio contact?" Bolan asked.

"There are a few formalities, Mr. Bolan," said Ling. "You'll just have to be patient."

Ling cut the intercom and left them with the scanner. Bolan was a nuisance, as the pilot had been. But they would all be taken care of soon.

The unloading was complete. The crates were stacked and the warehouse under armed guard. The laboratory was ready for testing under Dr. Lo.

Ling had sent for Lo Kim because he was the best biochemist available. Lo had already earned top honors for developing a drug that turned aggressive killers into mindless, docile children. State security had benefited from that. Now it was Ling's turn.

He was going to reproduce the germs. Ling knew what kind of power came to whoever controlled the germs. They were invisible. Impossible to trace. Selective. Quiet.

No one would spoil things for him. The radiation scare allowed him to isolate the witnesses. Now he was free to use them in Lo's tests. They would soon find out just how deadly these germs were.

They would start with Bolan.

The CIA station chief in Peking was agitated. There were always complications, but this was going to be trouble.

The lights went out, and then the newsreel came on, a ghostly glow in the dark. A Westerner looked out from the screen with hollow eyes. He read grimly in American-accented English from a paper on the table in front of him.

"My name is Mack Bolan. I am an American war criminal. For many years I have been paid by the bourgeois imperialists to kill in their cause.

"I have chosen of my own free will to defect to the People's Republic of China in the hope that through time I may wash the blood from my hands.

"I wish no further contact with the West or with agents of Western countries. I plan to join in the work of the people, anonymously if I can, and end my days in humble work.

"This is my final communiqué."

Bolan eyed the camera squarely until the Chinese interpreter caught up with him. Then the screen went dark.

The CIA station chief reached for the telephone.

MACK BOLAN LOOKED IN THE MIRROR. Something was bothering him, but he could not put his finger on it. All he knew was that he was different. His eyes and skin were different from other people's. He was much larger. He spoke with funny words and could not understand most of what other people said.

If he was different, why was he here with them?

He did not know how many weeks he'd been trying to figure that one out. The snow had melted outside the window, and still the doctors would not tell him.

Then the political-education classes started, and it took days and days of talking to the camera before he got it right for them. Why was it so hard? He still did not understand what an imperialist was.

There was a dog that stood on the roof across the way and stared at him. So Mack Bolan stopped eating. Maybe the dog would leave him alone.

And ever since he had stopped eating, he felt more and more different. The longer he went without food, the more different he felt.

Mack Bolan sat on the cot in his pajamas, trying to sort it all out. His head hurt to think so hard.

They then opened the door and helped his roommate to his bed. He was having trouble walking by himself. Bolan watched as they sat him on the edge of the bed. His eyes stared straight ahead, but there was no one home. Why did he have bandages on his temples?

Then they helped Bolan up and led him away the way they had led away his roommate.

Here was Dr. Ling. Nice doctor.

"So nice to see you, Bolan Mack," said Dr. Ling. "Are you going to get your clock fixed now?" He tapped Bolan's forehead. "That is very nice."

Bolan nodded but he was shy. They led him down the hall to a room. Bolan met the nice man in the room who ran the machine.

The nice men left. Bolan got up on the table as the nice man said. He wanted to do it right for him. The man showed him where to put his head so that it was between the metal clamps.

Bolan was looking up at the ceiling when the man's face appeared over him. He had a syringe in his hand.

Mack Bolan clamped his hands around the technician's neck and tightened them until the man choked.

Bolan rose over him until he was on top of him, choking the life out of him. The syringe dropped to the floor.

He was starting to remember.

Bolan dropped the technician to the floor and then taped his head. On the table he found the metal implements; he chose a spiked probe.

Mack Bolan lumbered out of the room like a zombie and wandered down the corridor. Far ahead, Ling walked on.

Bolan remembered the footprints in the snow.

This time he was going to make sure.

Ling passed the chairman's portrait in the corridor and smiled. There was power, and then there was power.

Then the spike hit his neck.

Ling's head was forced around. Bolan's eyes bored into him. Now he really looked crazy. Seriously crazy.

"Take me downstairs" was all Bolan said. Ling felt the spike jab slightly. A puncture of the carotid artery would leave him with seven seconds to live before he bled to death. Bolan knew the spot.

Ling nodded as best as he could. There would be a chance to get him later, he thought. Downstairs.

Ling used his card to pass them through security.

DR. LO WAS MORE THAN PLEASED. He was overjoyed. The neutralizing serum he had developed had earned him special favor with State Security. They had held a banquet for him with the highest party members and academics. Still, he had never dreamed he would rise so quickly to the top. This was the pinnacle. There was no more important work in the country than this biochemical reproduction.

He looked up from the table in the wet room. The orderlies were bagging the day's last test subject for the incinerator. This was the only subject that was missing his feet. Dr. Lo finished recording the results. The stuff worked, sure.

He had never seen anything that killed so well.

They would finish off the rest of the test subjects tomorrow. Lo was not sure that was necessary but Ling wanted it.

Lo was certain he could deduce the formula from what they already had. A couple of hours in his room and he was sure he would have it. He closed the precious folder to carry to his room.

Lo felt so close to solving it that his palms were sweating.

THE ELEVATOR OPENED in the basement. Ling stood with a patient. The patient's mind was gone, and he smiled blissfully with his hand on Ling's shoulder.

The security officer looked at the armed guards as if to say "Another one?" But the guards readied their keys for the metal door.

The guards passed them through.

That made five subjects in one day.

Bolan and Ling stood in the corridor. At one end was a lab where a man was working on some papers. In front of them was a windowed door to a storeroom. Machines hummed in the background.

Bolan took them into the storeroom and reconned quickly. The crates were very old and marked in Japanese. There were three doors: one to the lab, one to the corridor and one for the trucks to back in to unload.

Bolan was going to blow up this place, too. Just as he had blown up the caves.

Ling struggled now. He knew there was no place left to go.

Bolan held him tighter and ripped open the carotid with his spike, then stood back to avoid the pulsing jet of blood.

Bolan remembered a name now: the Executioner.

Quickly he unloaded a crate and smashed it to pieces. The splinters he disposed of under the row of pipes along the wall.

Ling was in the middle of the floor, twitching in a pool of blood. Bolan knocked for the guards. The first one stuck his head through the door and blinked in shock.

Bolan jerked him into the room and broke his neck. Before he dropped him he took the SMG. It was a make he had never seen before but there was one thing he knew immediately.

It felt good in his hands.

The second guard peeked in to see whether he was needed. Bolan blew him apart from hip to shoulder. The security guard ran for the stairs. Bolan cut him down.

Bolan took the guard's cigarette lighter and wiped the blood on his trousers. He spilled the fuel onto the pile of wood splinters he had built under the pipe system. He lit it and ran for the laboratory.

At the doorway he turned and blew the pipe apart. From the corner of his eye, Bolan saw the scientist disappear down a corridor. Then the room exploded.

Bolan flew down the corridor. The ceiling was ripping apart as he ran, dropping tiles and light fixtures in a flashing whirl of light. He saw the scientist turn a corner.

Bolan had an idea what he was carrying, and it frightened him.

The big guy rounded the corner to face two guards. The first he ripped apart from crotch to neck. Then he blew the other's brains out. No one was going to stop him now. He stole an extra magazine and slapped it into the SMG as he hit the stairs. Yeah. He knew what the scientist was carrying.

This one would not get away.

Bolan heard shouts. Up the stairwell he could see the white coat of the scientist and then the boots of the guards as they came to return fire.

Bolan stood on the landing and felt the good pump of the gun as he blew them all to hell. When he stopped there was only the smell of cordite and the screaming of the alarms. He could hear their cries as they converged on the stairwell. A dog was going crazy.

Bolan gathered up the file folder and shoved it inside his shirt. He slapped in another mag as he headed up the stairs. The building was pounding with the boots of the guards. He could see them on the railing as they came up from below.

Bolan hit the next floor at the same time the door flew inward. Bolan pounded the knot of guards in a furious death burst. Slugs ripped the cement open beside him. He swung off the railing and headed up. There was no thinking now, just adrenaline and the mad pumping of his heart.

As Bolan hit the top floor, a face appeared in the square of glass. Bolan pumped a round into it and looked up the flight of steps.

At the top was a door chained shut.

At the top was a door chained shut.

Bolan whirled and sprayed the doorway. Two more guards fell. One lay screaming as Bolan pivoted and blew apart the door chain.

In the split second that Bolan hit the sunlight the dog sprang. The hunger of the past few days had made her desperate. Her teeth sunk into his neck.

Bolan grabbed at the jaws as he fell with the dog on top of him. The animal growled and the adrenaline worked somewhere in the center of his being. He found the jaws and pulled with the leverage of his shoulders. The growl went up in pitch. Bolan felt the cartilage give as the jaws went slack. He had broken them.

Bolan sprang up and around. There was a copter.

Blood was ebbing down his chest but the adrenaline was pumping so fast he felt only numbness. He punched the start button with shaking hands and then turned to the stairwell door.

A guard poked his head around and Bolan sprayed it with fire. He had them pinned now—they could not get out on the roof without stepping into the Executioner's gunfire.

The rotors were whooshing more quickly, and Bolan felt the good surge that comes with victory. With the SMG trained on the doorway, Bolan climbed into the copter and lifted off. He pulled it up and then banked away from their fire. Bolan had the world by the balls. The whole wing of the institute was in flames.

He circled in the helicopter high enough to see the ocean. Maybe he could make Japan on this much fuel.

Over the coast, his adrenaline began to ebb and the pain grew. His neck was caked with blood where the dog had bitten him, but the major arteries were intact. His shoulder hurt, too, and he was remembering clinging to the underside of the copter. Every detail was coming back to him now.

But he was losing blood. His neck was still open. He was making time but all the while he felt weaker. His head felt faint; the thump of the rotors receded. Bolan shook his head to clear it. He had one more thing to do, even if it was his last.

Inside his shirt he found the folder. He held the stick between his knees. He had enough strength in his hands to tear it into smaller and smaller pieces. Bolan opened the door of the copter and tossed out the scraps.

He watched them fall like petals to the sea.

EPILOGUE

The hotel room was quiet. Brognola was in front of the television set when Bolan awoke. It was a police show of sorts; Bolan wasn't sure because they were speaking Japanese.

Brognola was having trouble with the food. He did not reconize any of it but he guessed that it was fish. He set it aside as Bolan rolled over and sat upright on the edge of the bed.

He was sore but healing. His neck was wrapped in bandages; it had taken thirty-three stitches to close the bite wound and he was in for a round of inoculations. The shoulder was almost normal. The time in Ling's institute had given it time to heal.

"We didn't know if you were coming back, Mack," said Brognola. "We knew about the bomb and we watched the explosion from our spy satellite, and then we didn't hear from you for weeks. Then that film of you saying you'd defected. I didn't believe it, of course, but I was worried."

"What film is that?"

"Jesus, you really were doped up, weren't you?"

"I can't remember much," said Bolan. "They were taking over my mind. If I hadn't stopped eating the food..."

Brognola was eating again. "Speaking of fright, are you sure Ling didn't reproduce them?"

Mack lay back down on the bed. "Oh, yeah. I blew the place up good. I took the formula myself."

"You took the formula? Where the hell is it?" Brognola stared at Bolan excitedly.

Bolan was deadpan. "I gave it to the cook downstairs," he joked.

MORE ADVENTURE NEXT MONTH WITH

MACK BOLAN

#85 Sunscream

For Export Only: Crime

The KGB makes an offer to the European Mafia that it cannot refuse: create a single worldwide syndicate in return for an unlimited arms supply.

The Russians believe that such a crime force would destabilize the West, paving the way for a Soviet takeover.

Mack Bolan poses as a German hit man to smash the evil alliance before it takes root.

What readers are saying about Gold Eagle books and Mack Bolan.

"There are no books about any person, nonfiction or fiction, that I like better than the Executioner series. Mack brings to life the longing of every law-abiding citizen."

*S.W., Christiansburg, VA

"I'm a woman sergeant in Army Intelligence and I thoroughly enjoy all your books. Mack is a fascinating, believable character representing so much in our world. Please don't change him!"

L.H., APO, NY

"These works are exactly what the world needs; they demonstrate in good-old-fashioned terms, the triumph of good over evil and sometimes at very good cost to the innocent. Mack's intrepid people are just what the doctor ordered."

Y.P., Plattsview, Nova Scotia

"I really must tell you you have created the most interesting series I've ever read. Bolan is the most exciting hero of our times."

H.R., Watertown, NY

"I hope you keep Mack going against the bad people of the world. I believe your books are the best."

J.K., FPO, Miami, FL

"I have read all the books and wouldn't trade them for anything. I love every page. Mack is the meaning of the word American and everything it should stand for."

W.S., APO, CA

"Gold Eagle books are all of the most superior reading—there is a hell of a lot of food for thought in each and every one. Gold Eagle is to be congratulated and commended for the type of books they publish."

M.C., Painted Post, NY

"All the Executioner books are super. Thanks."

M.D., Loveland, OH

"I have been a devoted reader of your books and I've enjoyed all of them. I thank you for writing the type of books that put forward the way things should be handled in this country."

C.S., Canplejeune, NC

"In my own mind, I cannot think of any books I've enjoyed more than yours."

E.D., Round Lake, IL

"We really think your writing is so realistic that it is hard to believe that your books are not based on real-life events."

C.J., NRM, Tempe, AZ

"I hope your books never stop."

D.L., Alliance, OH

"I'm in the Air Force, stationed overseas and if it wasn't for your books, it would be very hard for me here. I only have 9½ months left here and I can't wait to get back to the States to read all the ones I've missed."

N.W., APO, NY

Names available on request.

TAKE 'EM NOW

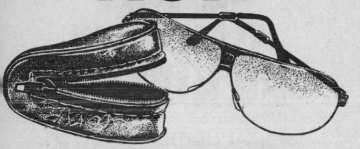

FOLDING SUNGLASSES
FROM GOLD EAGLE

Mean up your act with these tough, street-smart shades. Practical, too, because they fold 3 times into a handy, zip-up polyurethane pouch that fits neatly into your pocket. Rugged metal frame. Scratch-resistant acrylic lenses. Best of all, they can be yours for only $6.99. MAIL ORDER TODAY.

Send your name, address, and zip code, along with a check or money order for just $6.99 + .75¢ for postage and handling (for a total of $7.74) payable to Gold Eagle Header Service, a division of Worldwide Library. New York and Arizona residents please add applicable sales tax.

Remove from pouch..

unfold once..

unfold twice

and they're ready to wear

In USA:
2504 W. Southern Ave.
GOLD **Tempe, Arizona**
EAGLE **85282**

GES1

4 FREE BOOKS
1 FREE GIFT
NO RISK
NO OBLIGATION
NO KIDDING
